Gene leaned toward Sloane's attractive mouth, staring into her delicious dark eyes.

When she showed no desire to stop him, he planted a kiss on her awaiting luscious lips. Sloane opened her mouth almost immediately, allowing him to slip his tongue inside. Their tongues danced as they circled one another desirously.

Sloane sucked greedily on his lower lip as Gene flicked his tongue across her upper lip while the sexual sounds they were creating reverberated in his ears. Sloane's tongue whipped in and out of his mouth, teasing and tasting him while Gene pressed his lips to hers tightly in a feverish kiss that left him breathless yet wanting so much more. Sloane wrapped her hands around his head, opening her mouth wider and drawing him in with utter abandon.

The kiss continued unabated for several minutes and Gene became lost in Sloane and her swollen lips. She gave him another powerful kiss, then pulled back, releasing his head from her firm grip.

"Getting a bit toasty, isn't it?" she said with a smile.

"No complaints here," Gene said, leaning in to kiss her again.

Books by Devon Vaughn Archer

Kimani Romance

Christmas Heat
Destined to Meet
Kissing the Man Next Door
Christmas Diamonds
Pleasure in Hawaii

Kimani Arabesque

Love Once Again

DEVON VAUGHN ARCHER

is a bestselling author of romance and mainstream fiction. He became the first male author to write for Harlequin's Arabesque line with his groundbreaking mainstream romance, *Love Once Again,* in 2006.

He has gone on to write a number of scintillating romances for Harlequin's Kimani Romance line, including holiday romance classics, *Christmas Heat* and *Christmas Diamonds,* as well as *Dark and Dashing, Kissing the Man Next Door* and *Destined to Meet.*

The author's current romance, *Pleasure in Hawaii,* is the first novel in a Hawaii-based romance series Passions in Paradise. This will be followed by *Private Luau,* scheduled for publication in December 2011.

He also writes young-adult romance and mystery fiction, including a recent original Kindle ebook romance, *Her Teen Dream Guy.*

Devon resides in the Pacific Northwest, but is a frequent traveler to the Hawaiian Islands.

Connect with him through Facebook, MySpace and at www.devonvaughnarcher.com.

Devon Vaughn Archer

To my mother, Marjah Aljean, who has had a lifelong dream of going to Hawaii and can do so through the words and imagination within these pages.

And my father, Johnnie Henry, who has moved on to a better place in heaven, but is forever with us spiritually.

Recycling programs for this product may not exist in your area.

ISBN-13: 978-0-373-86215-3

PLEASURE IN HAWAII

www.kimanipress.com

Printed in U.S.A.

Dear Reader,

I am so excited to bring you the first book in my Passions in Paradise series, which presents a love story on three different islands of Hawaii. There is no more breathtaking, romantic setting for two people to discover one another and fall in love.

I chose Hawaii as the setting for a romance series because, as a regular visitor to the islands, it seemed like the perfect place to cultivate a romantic relationship amidst the palm trees, sandy beaches and other sights and sounds of paradise.

In *Pleasure in Hawaii,* the Island of Maui, known as the Valley Isle, is the idyllic backdrop for Gene and Sloane as chemistry and passion collide after a sneaker wave introduces the two.

Book 2 in the series, *Private Luau,* takes place on the Island of Oahu, and will be published in December 2011.

Happy reading!

Devon Vaughn Archer

Thanks to the entire staff at Kimani
for their role in bringing this contemporary romance to fruition—and particularly to Alex and Kelli, my editors.

Chapter 1

Awakening to the sounds of waves crashing, Sloane Hepburn couldn't help but smile. She had to pinch herself to believe she was actually living—not vacationing—in Maui, Hawaii. Sand. Sun. Ocean. Mountains. Palm trees. As much a paradise as anything she'd ever seen. Yet here she was, relocated from Raleigh, North Carolina, after getting promoted to director of guest relations at her company's grand resort hotel, Island Shores, located in Wailea on Maui's southern coast.

Leaving behind family and friends was not easy, but she would have been a fool to pass up the opportunity afforded her for career advancement. After all, wasn't that why she went to college and worked so hard? With no great love of her life keeping Sloane in Raleigh, the job had to come first. Besides, she was sure there were plenty of hot men as prospects in Maui, though she suspected the best ones were probably tourists and therefore not for her.

Sloane had been in Maui for only a few days and had yet to find a place to call home. Staying in a nice oceanfront suite at the hotel was satisfying, but she preferred keeping work and her private life separate.

After throwing on some running clothes and tying her long raven hair into a ponytail for a morning jog, Sloane left her seventh-floor room. When she got downstairs, she saw her boss in the lobby. Alan Komoda was the general manager of Island Shores.

"Good morning," he said in a cheery voice.

"Morning, Alan," Sloane said to the sixtysomething, white-haired Polynesian man, noting he was wearing his usual expensive dark suit. She felt a little self-conscious at being casually dressed instead of being in her business attire.

"Are you settling in all right on the island?"

"Yes, thanks. Maui is definitely agreeing with me."

"Good to know." His eyes crinkled. "We're happy to have you as part of our staff."

She blushed. "Works both ways."

"By the way, there's a large contingent coming in from Japan in two days. They love everything about the water, so I want to make sure we do whatever we can to make their visit unforgettable."

"I'll take care of it," Sloane assured him, already aware of the group. She had come up with some great water adventures for them.

Alan nodded and then waved her off as his cell phone rang.

Sloane left the hotel and soaked in the warm air as it hit her face, along with the humidity. Dawn had barely crept over the horizon. She walked the few steps to the beach, sucked in a deep breath, and began to run with the wind.

She'd been jogging since high school and couldn't think of a better way to work out and get her heart racing.

Well, maybe there was another way. She briefly imagined meeting a drop-dead gorgeous man and making sweet, passionate love to him all night long. That would certainly raise the blood pressure and temperature, while exercising every part of her body in an enjoyable manner.

Sloane felt herself getting hot from the thought in combination with the run and cleared her mind, preferring the real thing to imagination. She was jogging along the shoreline and barely cognizant of the rather large wave that seemed to come from nowhere. It slammed right into her, knocking Sloane onto her bottom, drenching her from head to toe.

For an instant, panic set in as Sloane actually wondered if she might be washed out to sea and lost forever. *I don't want to die.* The idea of her life ending tragically before it ever truly began had her head spinning. Then, as though her prayers had been answered, she felt powerful arms lift her straight up and onto wobbly legs.

Without taking the time to study this magnificent creature that stood firm in a coat of dark fudge armor, Sloane found her hands wrapping around his thick neck gratefully, hanging on for dear life as the wave disappeared from whence it came.

"Are you all right?" the profoundly masculine voice asked, sincere concern in his tone.

"I think so," Sloane said, realizing she was still hugging him. Part of her could have stayed that way forever, somehow feeling protected in knowing that his muscular arms were snuggled around her as well and apparently in no hurry to let her go. But the fact was the man was a total stranger and she was wet and sandy. Those factors forced

Sloane to pry her arms away from his hard body. "You can probably let me go now."

He complied with her request and honed in on her with incredibly sexy and deep gray-brown eyes. "No problem."

"I'm not sure what just happened..." she murmured.

"Looks like you were caught by a sneaker wave. I saw it coming and called out to you, but I guess the noise from the ocean drowned me out, so to speak."

Sloane colored under the weight of his gaze, which showed no hesitancy in wandering up and down her body as if sizing her up for the taking. She could feel the moist fabric of her clothing clinging to her every curve almost invitingly.

Well, two could play that game. She took a moment to assess her admittedly very nice-looking hero. He was, like her, in his early thirties. With a rich chocolate complexion, he was maybe six-three—bringing her head to his shoulders—with muscles threatening to rip from underneath his navy tank. He wore black mesh shorts, showing off runner's bulging quadriceps and long, sturdy legs tapering down to his bare feet. It was almost as though he were created entirely from her sexual fantasy, perfectly enticing from top to bottom.

Sloane blinked away such delicious thoughts as her eyes came up again to his. "Well, thanks for your help," she told him, feeling more than a little embarrassed. "I didn't realize the waves could come up so suddenly."

"There's usually more bark than bite to them," he suggested. "Had the wave decided to take you out for a ride, I would've come after you, believe me, and pulled you back to safety."

Oddly enough, Sloane believed every word, even if the

notion of placing her life in another person's hands, no matter how capable, unnerved her.

"So you're a lifeguard?" she asked. *And a very attractive one at that.*

He chuckled with a deep resonance, cheeks dimpling in the process. "Me, a lifeguard? I don't think so. Just someone who couldn't live with himself if a pretty lady was lost at sea and I was around to stop it from happening and didn't."

Sloane wasn't used to such a smooth operator. Not to mention one who was willing to put his life on the line for her. A pity he was likely only visiting Maui before heading back to who knew where. She wouldn't be surprised at all if his wife or girlfriend were waiting for him in their hotel room, eager for his company. After all, who came to Hawaii alone?

"Again, I appreciate your being around when you were."

"No big deal," he said coolly. "By the way, my name's Gene Malloy."

"Hi. I'm Sloane Hepburn."

"Nice to meet you, Sloane Hepburn."

"You too," she replied.

"Are you here on vacation?"

Sloane weighed how much she should tell someone she was likely to never see again. "My job brought me here."

His eyes widened with surprise. Or perhaps delight. "That so? What do you do?"

"I work in guest relations at a hotel."

"Sounds like interesting work."

"It is most of the time," she said.

"And the rest?"

Sloane smiled. "Tedious, but I'm not complaining." She was surprised how easily she could talk to him. Did he have that effect on all women? Or only those sopping-wet from a sneaker wave?

"Of course not," Gene said, clearly amused.

"So what about you?" she wondered.

"What about me?"

"Are you on holiday?"

He gave her a lopsided grin. "You could say I'm on holiday 24/7. Or damned near."

She raised a brow. "You mean you're independently wealthy and go wherever you want to?"

"Not exactly." Gene turned around and pointed to a cluster of palm trees just beyond the beach. "I run a bed-and-breakfast up there. It keeps me on my toes, but I don't consider it work per se."

Sloane would never have imagined this marvelous specimen of a man to be the owner of a bed-and-breakfast—and in Maui, no less. One just never knew these days. She wondered if he ran it alone or with a special lady in his life.

Deciding they had probably already taken up too much of each other's time and wanting to go shower off the sand, Sloane met Gene's enticing eyes. "I'd better let you get back to your bed-and-breakfast."

"Probably a good idea," he agreed. "My guests can get restless when breakfast is not on time."

She smiled, trying to picture him cooking for a group. Or did the breakfast side of his establishment consist of mainly cereal, fruit and nuts?

"Have a nice day," she told him.

"You, too. And stay away from those sneaker waves.

Sloane flushed. "I'll try my best."

She started running back toward the hotel, turning briefly to see Gene walking up the beach. He was looking her way and raised a long arm to wave. She waved back, hoping this wouldn't be the last time they saw each other.

Or was she hoping for too much, considering that Gene Malloy likely had much more on his mind than rescuing damsels in distress? Even if this one found him to be utterly handsome and the type of man she could imagine cuddling under the sheets with for some hot fun and frolic. Just because she was married to her job, in a manner of speaking, didn't mean she had to live like a nun in Maui. Especially if the right man happened to materialize and was also looking for a nonserious but very romantic fling.

Gene Malloy was tempted to follow the striking lady named Sloane Hepburn like a lust-struck puppy. But he thought better of it. As much as he would love to take her to bed and get to know her in every intimate way possible, it probably wasn't going to happen. Having been married once with damned near disastrous results, he wasn't looking to jump back into a serious relationship in the foreseeable future. Sloane struck him as someone who wasn't into casual sex. Or did he have her pegged wrong?

Gene stopped in his tracks and watched as Sloane continued to put some distance between them. Every morning he liked to come out on the beach, soak in the atmosphere, and get ready for another day in paradise. The last thing he expected to see before his very eyes was a beautiful woman running way too close to the water, practically asking it to knock her down on her lovely tush.

Well, she got her wish. He could see that she was shaken up about the whole thing, as though the ocean would have swallowed her up whole. Though that was never going to happen, it had given him a good excuse to come over and help her out while getting an up-close look. He wasn't disappointed in the least.

Sloane was easily the most attractive woman he'd seen in some time. Long and silky wet coal-colored hair cascaded down her back and bordered a heart-shaped face. Bold sable eyes captivated him beneath thin brows, and a dainty nose perched over her pouty lips. Her skin shade was like melted sweet caramel, and her slender body oozed sex appeal beneath the red fitness bra and blue athletic shorts. He imagined those long, shapely legs wrapped around his waist while they made frenetic love.

Taking looping strides, Gene crossed the beach and came upon Malloy's Bed and Breakfast. He'd purchased the remodeled 1930s two-story plantation home in a quiet residential area in Wailea four years ago with his then-wife, Lynda. It was supposed to be their dream come true to turn the place into the perfect getaway for travelers to Maui. But the dream became a nightmare when Lynda grew homesick and decided she was better off without him or the bed-and-breakfast. She returned to their hometown of Detroit and filed for divorce.

Gene had known that they were drifting apart for a while, but had hoped the relocation to Maui and away from family influences might be enough to save the marriage. All it did was prolong the inevitable. Now he was on his own and determined to keep the bed-and-breakfast running and profitable. Things were looking pretty good on both counts at the moment.

Having someone new in his life was something Gene would definitely welcome, so long as the person understood that his priority these days was playing host to his guests. Most women weren't secure enough to play second fiddle. He wondered if Sloane Hepburn was any different. Or had her business relocation also had a romantic element to keep her company at night?

After brushing off the sand that Sloane had passed his way when he lifted her up and they held each other, Gene went in the back door. He didn't see any of the guests up and at it yet, which suited him just fine. It would only take a few minutes to get breakfast ready.

In the gourmet kitchen, Gene glanced around at its Euro-style cabinetry, engineered stone countertops, butcher-block center island, and Sub-Zero wine refrigerator before washing his hands. He sliced up locally grown organic pineapple, papayas, mangoes and strawberries. He placed the fruit on a platter and then got out cereal, yogurt, granola, bagels, muffins and macadamia nuts. This was followed by tropical juices, assorted teas and fresh-ground Maui-grown coffee.

He began setting things out on the covered lanai, surrounded by coconut palm trees and adorned with orange and purple bougainvillea, expecting the guests to show up at any moment.

Gene paused, taking stock of his bed-and-breakfast. There were four guest suites, each designed with its own theme that reflected the island: Ocean Suite, Beach Suite, Garden Suite, and Paradise Suite. Currently only the Paradise Suite was unoccupied, until the guests arrived later this afternoon.

Gene was happy to handle most everything himself these days, with some occasional assistance from Dayna Yee, a Filipino woman who lived down the street and had once run her own bed-and-breakfast with her husband until he died a decade ago. Tapping into his marketing background, Gene had been able to effectively promote the business on the internet and various other travel sources, to make sure Maui-bound travelers and even locals looking for a little escape from the norm were aware of Malloy's Bed and Breakfast as a welcoming place for all.

Gene's thoughts returned briefly to Sloane, remembering how good she'd felt in his arms. Her skin was so soft and her body lithe, with bends and folds in all the right places, seemingly made just for him. He would rescue her any day, anytime. He was sure they could create their own fireworks were the opportunity to ever present itself.

"Something smells really good," Judith Westchester said, entering the lanai with her husband, Brook.

Gene grinned, watching the seventyish couple approach him. "That would be the coffee," he told her, breathing in the aroma himself. "Grown right here in the West Maui Mountains. Only the freshest and very best for my guests."

"That's what we like to hear," Brook Westchester said, touching his glasses.

"Help yourself," Gene said, raising his hand. "You'll find everything you need to start your day."

"In that case, we'll dig in," Judith said.

Soon other guests filtered in and had breakfast en route to making the most of their stay on the island with various activities, some arranged by Gene. By eleven o'clock, he had put the dishes in the dishwasher, cleaned up, and pretty much had the rest of the day to himself. It gave him plenty of time to think about that lovely lady named Sloane, who had practically materialized before his eyes, as if from the sea itself.

It was past noon when Sloane, dressed professionally in a silver skirt suit and matching sandals, greeted guests arriving at the Island Shores Resort.

"Aloha," she said warmly to a young couple who seemed

hopelessly in love, placing traditional flower leis over their heads.

"Aloha!" they said back excitedly.

Sloane gave them a big smile, wanting all the guests to feel at home and prepare to have the time of their lives. She could only imagine what it must be like to be in love with someone and share that affection on the island of Maui, where everything was so beautiful and idyllic. Maybe someday she would get to find out, assuming such a man would enter her life and they could both fully commit themselves to each other.

Her mind wandered to an hour earlier when telling her colleague and new friend, Kendra Arquette, about her scary and exhilarating experience on the beach.

"I never saw the wave coming," she related. "If my hero hadn't come along when he did, who knows what might have happened…"

Kendra, who had worked at the hotel for a year since moving to Hawaii from Illinois, leaned forward over the front desk. "No reason to even go there. Besides, from what you tell me, this hottie hunk you've described would never have let you drown."

"So he says."

"Looks like he backed it up with action. Lucky you." Kendra smiled, brushing her long brown yarn braids away from her face. "Why can't I ever have a gorgeous guy drop everything to save me?"

Sloane chuckled while feeling a tad guilty. *Maybe I should've done more to show my appreciation.* "I suppose I should find a way to properly thank him for being a gentleman and coming to my rescue."

"You said he runs a bed-and-breakfast, right?"

"Yes." Sloane couldn't help but wonder if he was as

thorough in bed as he was in the sand. “But I couldn’t just intrude—”

“Why not?” Kendra asked.

“Well, for one, his wife or girlfriend might not approve.”

“Who says he has a wife or girlfriend?”

Sloane fluttered her lashes. “A good-looking man like that running a bed-and-breakfast in Maui all by himself? I don’t think so.”

“You won’t know unless you go,” Kendra advised. “Besides, it’s not as if you’re trying to marry the man. Or are you?”

Sloane laughed. “Oh, no. Marriage is the furthest thing from my mind these days.” Something short of that might work, assuming they were on the same page. That had rarely been the case from past experiences. Most men wanted, even expected, everything while offering something far less.

“Well, then, you have nothing to lose. Even if there is someone in his life, you might make another friend. Or two.”

“You’re right,” Sloane decided. “I’ll give it a shot.” Hopefully, she wouldn’t regret intruding upon his life.

Sloane’s thoughts returned to the present. Maybe she would see Gene again on the beach tomorrow. That way she wouldn’t make either of them uncomfortable by showing up at his bed-and-breakfast and perhaps making a fool of herself.

She put on a bright smile as a family of four entered the hotel’s lobby. “Aloha,” she said warmly, placing a flower lei around each of their necks. “Welcome to the Island Shores Resort.”

Chapter 2

Sloane kept her distance from the water as she did her morning jog. Her unfortunate mishap had forced her to cut it short yesterday. Not that she had a problem being scooped up into the muscular arms of Gene Malloy. He'd seemed to enjoy it every bit as much. And maybe that was a bad thing for both of them, if his attention should have been directed elsewhere.

Sloane had done a little research on Gene's business. It wasn't too difficult to locate Malloy's Bed and Breakfast on the internet. It had been in business for four years and had won several awards for hospitality. There was a small picture of Gene's handsome face on his web page and no indication of whether or not he was truly operating it alone. Perhaps his wife or girlfriend had chosen to keep a low profile.

Either way, Sloane was determined to make good on her desire to thank Gene once more. When she reached the area where the wave had hit her, she looked around for Gene but didn't see him anywhere. A tiny streak of disappointment whizzed through her, as if he should be at her beck and call. The reality was that he had better things to do than hang around in hopes that she might show up again.

Sloane looked up toward the bed-and-breakfast, which sat on a hill and offered a nice view of the ocean. She was having second thoughts about making contact with him again after they had already said their goodbyes. Would she give him the wrong impression by showing up there?

Never being known for backpedaling once she had made up her mind, Sloane sprinted across the sand and up some steps. She marveled at the rectangular plantation house. It was alabaster and embodied the Southern country manor, neoclassical and Greek revival styles she had always admired in magazines with its low-pitched roof, soaring columns and tall French windows bordered by black wooden shutters. When she was a little girl, Sloane had imagined living in such a house.

She stepped onto the lanai and was about to knock on the half-glass, stained front door when it opened. A young couple stood there in matching colorful outfits.

"Aloha," they said.

Sloane smiled. "Aloha."

They came out and skipped along on their way. Sloane went in and stepped onto the hickory hardwood floor. The interior was open and roomy, with a blend of antique and contemporary furnishings. Some hanging spider and Swedish ivy plants gave the interior a homey feel.

An attractive dark-skinned woman in her thirties approached Sloane. "Hi. Are you looking for Gene?"

Sloane wondered if she was his wife. "Yes, I am. I just wanted to—"

"There he is," the woman interrupted as Gene walked in from the kitchen. "I think another guest has arrived."

"Sloane—" His tone and wide-eyed look told her that he clearly wasn't expecting to see her in his establishment.

The woman smiled at Sloane and turned to Gene with a little wave. "Be back later. Have fun."

Sloane watched her leave the house before facing Gene. Like the day before, he was a sight for sore eyes, and he seemed just as taken by her. She liked the way he smelled of a nice woodsy-type cologne.

"Hey," he said, smoothing a thick eyebrow.

"Hi." Sloane felt slightly awkward but hoped it didn't show.

"What are you doing here?"

"I just wanted to check out your bed-and-breakfast," she told him as the first thing that popped into her head. "Hope you don't mind?"

His amazing eyes creased at the corners. "Not at all. You're more than welcome."

"Thanks." Sloane paused, thinking this was a good start. "I've never been in a bed-and-breakfast before."

"I'll be happy to show you around. It's a cool place to stay for anyone who wishes to enjoy the surroundings in a down-to-earth, family-friendly-type atmosphere."

She lifted a brow playfully. "You mean unlike at the big resort hotels?"

He grinned. "Didn't say that. Different strokes for different folks. Some people prefer big, extravagant, expensive places for their vacation. Others want a more relaxed, laid-back place that won't take much of a bite out of their wallet."

Sloane couldn't argue with that. The reality was, she actually would have preferred more modest trappings had she been there as a vacationer, especially with the host being so appealing and sexy.

She gazed up at him. "So, was that woman who just left your wife or…?"

"No," Gene said, jutting his chin. "Her name is Ngozi. She's a guest from Tanzania. I'm not married, divorced actually, and not currently seeing anyone."

"Oh." Sloane tried to pretend to be nonchalant at the news. *I never would have imagined a man like you would be available.*

Gene angled his eyes upon her. "How about you?"

"Single, never married."

"So the right fellow has never come along?" he asked curiously.

Sloane considered whether this was the right time to explain that her priorities often left her with little time for romance. "With my work, I haven't had the time to get serious about anyone," she told him candidly.

"I see."

"Do you?"

"Yeah," he said. "Career-oriented person. There's nothing wrong with that."

Sloane met his eyes. "Sounds like you're leaning that way yourself these days." Or was she misreading between the lines?

"Guess I am," Gene acknowledged. "Trying to run a bed-and-breakfast alone can be a full-time thing, at least where it concerns putting most of my energy."

Sloane got his drift. He wasn't looking to settle down with anyone again. That suited her just fine, as that wasn't what she needed from a man at this time in her life.

Ten minutes later she had been escorted through the entire house and was impressed with its structure and the different themes for each room. Obviously much forethought had gone into the design, which told Sloane just how committed Gene was to his bed-and-breakfast. And apparently it was paying off. She met a couple of the guests, who couldn't seem to say enough about Gene's hospitality. Sloane felt a bit envious and only hoped the guests under her watch at the hotel would have such satisfaction during their stay.

She and Gene ended up on a shady lanai surrounded by tropical flowers, a rock garden and a fountain. It seemed like the perfect place for Sloane to say what she came to tell him.

"I wanted to thank you for helping me on the beach yesterday by buying you lunch tomorrow," she said, "if you're available."

Gene grinned. "It's not necessary to pay in thanking me, but I'd be happy to have lunch with you tomorrow."

"It's the least I can do," she explained, "even if it's not necessary."

"I understand, and it works for me."

He was close enough to Sloane that she could feel his warm breath on her cheeks, exciting her.

"Can you meet me at the Island Shores Resort Coconut Café around noon?" she asked.

Gene playfully mulled it over. "I think I can fit that into my day. I'll be there."

Sloane found herself transfixed by his wide and inviting mouth, wanting more than anything to kiss him. Would he object, or were they not on the same wavelength? *Am I seriously contemplating such a bold move?*

"Good," she said, having second thoughts about the kiss and losing her nerve. "I'll get back to my run now and out of your hair, so to speak."

Gene gave a low, sexy laugh and ran a hand across the

top of his smooth head. "If I had any hair up there, you'd be welcome to it."

"Oh, would I?" Sloane met his eyes invitingly.

"Anytime." He grabbed a few tendrils of her hair. "You've got beautiful hair. I'd love to run my fingers through it sometime."

She liked the idea of his long fingers caressing her hair and her body. "Maybe I'll let you one day," she replied.

He moved ever so close and rolled his fingers across and inside her hair, gently massaging Sloane's scalp. "Feel good?"

"Yes," she admitted, her head tingling.

Gene stopped and held her chin. "What would you do if I kissed you right now?"

Sloane quivered at the thought, but did not back away. "Guess you'd have to try it to find out."

"I never was one to resist a challenge," Gene said levelly.

He tilted his head slightly and planted a soft kiss on Sloane's mouth. It was short, but very sweet.

"Nice," she told him, licking her lips and tasting his. "We'll have to try that again sometime."

His dimples deepened. "Whenever you wish."

"Goodbye, Gene."

"A hui hou," he said. "Or until we meet again."

Sloane smiled at his apparent mastery of the Hawaiian language. She walked away, glancing over her shoulder at him and receiving a confident grin in return.

Gene was still thinking about that kiss two hours later as he cleaned the house while his guests were out and about. He wanted to keep the place pristine at all times, while perfecting the technique of keeping a low profile when doing his chores. Just one peck on those ruby lips told him

Sloane Hepburn was someone he wanted to kiss a lot more. And since she seemed willing to explore the possibilities in a nonserious manner, he felt that they might be good for each other, in bed and out.

But he didn't want to jump too far ahead of himself. Obviously Sloane was a businesswoman first and foremost, as evidenced by her relocating to Hawaii for work. Still, he wanted to tap into the sexy woman within that could keep up with the sexy man inside him when not playing host at a bed-and-breakfast.

Gene found himself getting hot and bothered while picturing a naked Sloane on top of him while they burned the sheets in raw unbridled sex. He wondered who would tire first. Or would they both have an inexhaustible sex drive that needed to be satisfied?

When his latest arrivals, Harold and Stella Frasier, came in, Gene put his sexual thoughts on the back burner for now.

"How was the Maui Ocean Center Aquarium?" he asked them.

"It was wonderful," Stella said animatedly. "We saw humpback whales, bottlenose dolphins, devil scorpionfish, plus lots of other marine life."

"Yeah, we loved it," seconded Harold, who was probably ten years his wife's junior. "I thought the Hawaiian spiny lobsters were particularly interesting. Thanks for recommending the aquarium."

"It's a must for anyone visiting Maui," Gene bragged. "I'm glad you enjoyed it."

"Now we've built up a big appetite for lunch," Stella said. "Any suggestions for a great seafood restaurant?"

Gene nodded. "I think I might have a suggestion or two."

He finished his chores and went for a walk on the beach.

As usual, it was brimming with both locals and tourists, catching the sun's rays and the mesmerizing beauty of the Pacific Ocean. But what he most wanted to see was Sloane's gorgeous face. Of course, it was too much to expect that she would still be hanging around on the beach with her work and other activities.

Gene couldn't help but be smitten by the woman who had gotten a surprise from the water but still managed to look sexy as hell while wet and sandy. She'd looked even nicer today. He fully expected to get to know her better and see if they could find even more interesting ways to spend time together.

"So you're doing lunch with Mr. Bed-and-Breakfast," Kendra said to Sloane as they walked through the enormous hotel lobby the next morning.

"Yes, do you have a problem with that?" Sloane joked.

"Not at all." Kendra laughed. "We can all use more friends, right? Especially ones who are gorgeous and unattached, as you've described him."

"I agree, new friends in a new place is important. Those other qualities can't hurt things any, either." Sloane chuckled. "It doesn't mean I'm looking to hook up or anything."

"Maybe not, but there's more to Maui than catering to the needs of others. You're entitled to some fun and frolic. We both are."

"True," Sloane said, while not committing to anything as far as Gene Malloy was concerned. Admittedly, though, it was hard to ignore the stirring kiss he'd laid on her. Though it had only lasted a few seconds, the effect still had her reeling and imagining just what this man could do to her if she allowed him to. "Right now, I just plan to treat him to lunch and call it even for his coming to my aid."

Kendra smiled broadly. "Be sure to let me know if there's any dessert."

Sloane laughed. "You're too much. If the dessert is sweet enough, I promise you'll be the first to know. Now, we'd both better get to work."

"Don't remind me."

Sloane moved in a different direction. She checked her folder and then spotted the party she was looking for. There were ten Japanese visitors on a combined business-and-pleasure trip. She had made arrangements for them to go deep-sea fishing and snorkeling and to take a submarine tour.

She walked up to the group cheerfully. "I trust that the water activities I set up are to your satisfaction?"

"Very much so," said Jim Lee, with the others echoing his sentiments.

"That's good," she said. "If you need help with anything else to make your stay comfortable, don't hesitate to ask."

A thirtysomething female member of the group walked up to Sloane. "I'm Yoko," she said. "Can you arrange a helicopter tour for me? I'd love to take some pictures of the valleys and waterfalls."

Sloane smiled. "Sure, I'd be happy to take care of that for you." It sounded pretty adventurous and was something she hoped to be brave enough to do one day.

Gene stepped inside the Island Shores hotel for the first time since staying there when he and his ex had arrived in Maui four years ago. He'd forgotten how lavish the place was. Not that he didn't have plenty of reminders, as their TV and print ads dwarfed his own advertising budget. But what he lacked in cold hard cash, he made up for in determination and good old-fashioned hospitality with a personal touch that no resort hotel could ever hope to match. He had to admit, though, having the lovely Sloane as their guest relations director probably didn't hurt matters any if she were half as committed to the job as he suspected.

Making his way past a group of tourists, Gene entered the Coconut Café. He scanned the crowded place looking for his date. At least he considered it a date, even if she called it a thank-you lunch.

"Aloha." He heard the familiar voice from behind.

Gene turned and was blown away by Sloane. It was the first time he'd seen her professionally dressed, wearing a light blue two-button notched-collar pantsuit and pink wedges. Her hair was in a loose bun and she wore little makeup, which actually accentuated her fine features.

A grin formed on his face. "Back at you."

"Hope you weren't waiting too long," she said. "I got tied up in a meeting."

"Not a problem." Indeed, he found her well worth the wait. "I've only been here for a couple of minutes and was just gazing at the tourists."

Her mouth curved upward. "Shall we get a table?"

"Lead the way."

Gene followed her to a table with an ocean view. The waitress handed them menus.

"I'm going to have the grilled veggie sandwich," Sloane said without opening her menu. "Their ahi tuna and baked mahimahi are both excellent choices."

"Both sound delicious," Gene admitted, glancing at the menu. "I'll go with the mahimahi."

The waitress took their order after filling their glasses with water.

In a moment of silence, Gene couldn't help but think that even with such a magnificent seascape, the lady across from him was an even better attraction. And she had the most kissable mouth, with just the right amount of lip gloss.

"So this must be stepping out of your element," Sloane remarked, snapping him out of his reverie.

Gene chuckled. "Not really. I've spent my fair share of time at five-star resort hotels."

"But obviously you prefer the more intimate setting of the bed-and-breakfast?"

"I suppose I do," he conceded. "There's something about feeling at home even while on vacation that agrees with me. My guests feel the same way. But I'm sure those who prefer the big hotels can enjoy themselves every bit as much."

"Glad to hear you say that," she said. "Our guests love losing themselves in the lap of luxury."

Gene imagined her sitting on his lap, spurring pangs of desire. "And what about you? Have you lost yourself in this place?"

Sloane gave a cute laugh. "No, I haven't. For me, it's a job, though one I take great pride in. Truthfully, if I were here as a vacationer, I'd much rather stay in a quaint little bed-and-breakfast without too much excitement and noise."

He took note of that. "If you ever need to get away from it all, I'm sure I can find a spot for you to chill in my house."

"I'm sure you could," Sloane said with a lilt to her voice. "But I wouldn't want to be a distraction for you and your guests."

Gene grinned. "Quite the contrary, I think you would fit right in."

"You would say that."

"I never say what I don't mean," he told her.

"I believe you." Sloane tasted the water and ran her

tongue across her upper lip. “I might just take you up on that offer someday. You never know.”

Gene loved how she seemed to be a natural flirt. Just like him. It made him even more intrigued by her and the wonderful possibilities that existed between them.

Sloane gazed at Gene across the table, thinking it was nice to have him on her turf. She’d love to run her hands across that sexy bald head of his. He wore a short-sleeved pumpkin-colored polo shirt, his muscled arms on full display across the table.

“Where are you from?” she asked, dabbing the corners of her mouth with a napkin. She suspected from his accent that Gene was from the Midwest.

“Detroit,” he told her, and forked a piece of fish. “How about you?”

“Raleigh.”

“And I thought I was a long way from home,” Gene said with a laugh.

“I think we both are,” Sloane stated. “How did you come to choose Maui for your bed-and-breakfast?”

“My ex and I were looking to get out of the Motor City and try something different.” Gene paused, leaning back. “We’d vacationed once in Maui and fell in love with the atmosphere. Seemed like the perfect place to run our own bed-and-breakfast.”

“So what happened to make you go solo with the B&B, if you don’t mind my asking?” Or should she be minding her own business?

“I don’t mind,” he said coolly, running a hand across his head. “To be honest, you’re not the first person to wonder why I’m operating the B&B all by my lonesome.” He sipped iced tea and met her gaze. “Well, Lynda decided this wasn’t for her. Coupled with the fact that we hadn't been getting along very well, that was the end of the marriage."

"I'm sorry to hear that," Sloane told him, though she was sure he'd heard the same thing a thousand times.

"Don't be." He pinched the tip of his nose. "Some things aren't meant to be over time. You get over it and move on."

"I can relate to that," she admitted. "Not the marriage, but being involved in a relationship that wasn't meant to be."

Gene eyed her pensively. "He wanted a commitment and you didn't, or what?"

Sloane wondered if he was a mind reader. Or had she been that transparent in what she'd revealed about herself?

"Something like that," she responded.

"Oh yeah, the job comes first, right?"

She fluttered her lashes self-consciously. "Is that a bad thing?"

"Not from where I sit," Gene said, leaning toward her. "You have to do what you have to do. If a man can't deal with it, that's on him."

Sloane was starting to like Gene Malloy more and more, as he truly seemed to understand her without passing judgment. And vice versa. Maybe this new friendship could go somewhere.

"I suppose you must get guests from all over the world?" she asked, preferring to talk about him and the life he'd created in South Maui.

"Pretty much. I've had guests from Africa, England, Australia, China, Canada, the Bahamas, Mexico, Brazil and many of the states, including Alaska."

"Wow. I'm impressed."

Gene chuckled. "If you give the people what they want

in a getaway, they'll come back and spread the word to others. It's a win-win for everyone."

"But mostly for you," she suggested. "It means you're doing a good job and it's obviously paying off for you big-time."

"It is if you mean that I have a steady flow of guests year-round. But I'll never get rich as the owner of a bed-and-breakfast. It was never about the money, though. I get fulfillment in making sure that no one leaves disappointed."

Sloane could see why his guests were satisfied. She could probably learn a thing or two from him about that. And beyond the business side. Something told her that he was good at getting whatever—or whomever—he put his mind to.

"I'm glad that you put your guests first," she said, sipping her drink.

Gene favored her with a straight look. "Don't you?"

"Absolutely. As director of guest relations, it's my job to cater to our guests' needs and wants."

He nodded. "From what I saw in the lobby, you have a lot of guests to please."

Sloane grinned. "True, but I think I'm up to the task, even if at times some of them can be rather challenging."

Gene laughed. "Tell me about it. That's true whether you have many or hardly any guests. You just have to deal with them and keep a smile on your face."

"I couldn't have said it better myself," Sloane admitted, breaking into a big smile, knowing he expected it.

"Have you had the chance to go to a Maui luau yet?" Gene asked, putting a napkin to his mouth.

"As a matter of fact, I haven't. We have our own at the hotel, but between work and looking for a place to live, I haven't had the time."

"They have a great luau on Kaanapali Beach nightly. I was thinking about heading over there tonight and checking it out." He peered at her through those deep eyes. "And I could definitely use some company."

Sloane couldn't escape the heat of his gaze. "Are you asking me out on a date?"

Gene angled his face. "Yeah, I am, if you can find the time in your busy schedule. I know it's short notice, but you could probably use a break. I know I can. Also, it would give you a chance to see another part of Maui other than Wailea."

Sloane had to admit that the man could be very persuasive in hitting the right notes. It did sound like fun, and she could use the distraction from what had quickly become her normal and demanding routine. Besides, she welcomed the opportunity to spend more quality time with someone who seemed as interested as she was. Not to mention sexy and extremely good-looking.

"You're on," she told him.

Gene smiled broadly. "Great. Where are you staying?"

"Temporarily, I've got a room here." Sloane wished she had her own place instead of a hotel room. "The room was thrown in as part of the job."

"I have a great suite available," Gene offered, "should you need a respite from the noise, crowded elevators and touristy surroundings."

Sloane wondered if he was referring to his private suite. She could only imagine what type of personal service she could get from him there. Or might it be beyond her vivid imagination?

"Thanks for letting me know," she told him. "But I don't expect to be here much longer than another day or two. I have a couple of places I'll be looking at tomorrow."

"That's cool," Gene said. "Just thought I'd put the invite out there."

"It was sweet. Thank you." Sloane gave him a sincere smile and glanced discreetly at her watch. "Well, I'd better be getting back to work." *Believe me, I wish I could stay longer to talk to you.*

"Same here," Gene said. "There's always something that needs to be done at the house."

After Sloane paid for the lunch, they walked out into the lobby.

"I'll pick you up at seven," Gene told her.

"I'll be ready," Sloane promised, even if she had a lot to do between then and now. It was worth making the time to have some fun with someone who was clearly interested in getting to know her. The feeling was mutual.

Sloane wasn't sure if it would be awkward when they said their goodbyes. But Gene gave her a gentlemanly kiss on the cheek and was on his way without fanfare. She admired his firm and enviable backside for a moment before walking in the opposite direction. Sloane's hand made its way to her cheek where Gene's tender mouth had been, sending ripples of pleasure throughout her body.

Chapter 3

"Was that him?" Kendra asked, peering across the lobby through her glasses as Gene exited the hotel.

Sloane saw no use denying it. "Yep, sure was."

"Definitely hot!"

"Definitely," Sloane admitted.

"And he's definitely got his eye on you!"

"Maybe." Sloane didn't want to get too carried away too soon. "Time will tell."

"Seems like time has already told," Kendra said with a laugh. "You go from a romantic beach rescue to finding out that you're both available to have lunch at the best café in Wailea. One can only wonder what's next."

Sloane chuckled as they walked. "Well, wonder no longer. Gene's taking me to a luau tonight on Kaanapali Beach."

"Wow. I've been there—it's a great experience."

"So I've heard."

"Looks like you two are becoming an item," Kendra stated.

"We're just friends," Sloane told her, trying to keep it real at this point.

"That's what they all say. If this keeps up, it will be friends with some very nice benefits before you know it."

Sloane colored. "We won't talk about that. Right now, I'm just enjoying his company." Not to say that she wasn't up for nice and fulfilling benefits with someone who seemed to have an abundance of them.

Later Sloane was in her office working with her twenty-something assistant, Mia Makaiwi.

"We have Mr. and Mrs. Jonathan Washington arriving next week for their honeymoon," Sloane told her. "Aside from the usual lei greeting and bottle of wine, I'd like to add a few extra perks to their suite, like some rose petals leading up to the bed and chocolate macadamia nuts."

"Will do," Mia said, taking notes.

"Let's also throw in a volcano air tour that they might enjoy as newlyweds."

Mia's eyes lit up. "I went on that once. It was scary, but fun being up there in the twin-engine plane to see the rain forests and coastline of Maui."

"I'll have to try it myself someday if I ever get up the nerve," Sloane said. She pictured herself going on such an adventure with Gene, who seemed so steady and sure of himself.

"There's a class reunion here next month," Mia informed her. "I think it's a twenty-five-year reunion."

"That's great." Sloane loved planning such events. "Get me everything on it. I'll contact their representative and see if we can't help them do it right. Perhaps we can combine their class theme with a distinctively Hawaiian element."

"Good idea. They might as well take full advantage of being in Hawaii."

"Exactly." Sloane jotted down some notes. "Also, remind me that I'm supposed to put together an itinerary for Sally Weincroft, a seventy-five-year-old Australian who's flying in next month and wants us to decide how she should best spend her time during her first visit to America."

"That should be interesting," Mia said.

Sloane chuckled. "Challenging might be a better word. I want the experience to be memorable without seeming like it's just something for old folks to enjoy."

"Everyone enjoys everything in Hawaii, no matter the age," joked Mia.

"So it seems." Sloane had certainly learned since being there that most visitors seemed open to any experience in Maui, as though its majestic landscape caused inhibitions and fears to disappear. Perhaps she would apply this logic when carving out an agenda for Sally Weincroft.

Sloane imagined it could even work in her personal life as she navigated the waters of being single while still wanting to have a rewarding intimate involvement with no binding strings attached. This immediately caused thoughts of Gene to pop into her head.

"Yes, the first week of August is open in the Paradise Suite," Gene told the caller, Jean Hourdes. She was calling from Connecticut and had apparently narrowed her search of accommodations down to two places.

"Terrific," she said. "In that case, I'd like to make my reservation."

"Consider it done." He took down her credit card information gratefully.

"How's the weather there in August?" she wondered. "Or is it perfect year-round?"

"It's paradise," Gene said, sidestepping any mention of the rainy days. "August is actually our warmest month of the year, with temperatures usually in the low eighties with plenty of sunshine and steady trade winds to keep the temperatures from seeming too hot."

"I like it," Jean said animatedly.

Gene chuckled. "I knew you would. Well, you're all set, and I look forward to welcoming you to Maui and Malloy's Bed-and-Breakfast."

After Gene hung up, he saw Dayna Yee come into the small upstairs room he had set up as his office. She was in her early sixties, with fine white hair and cheeks dotted with tiny moles.

"Another guest will be arriving?" she asked after overhearing the conversation.

"Yes, in three weeks," he replied.

"The landscape people are coming this afternoon instead of tomorrow due to a scheduling conflict."

"I'll make a note."

"Oh, and the Foresters canceled their October booking," Dayna said.

Gene frowned. "Too bad. Did they give any reason why?"

She nodded. "They decided to spend their fiftieth anniversary closer to home."

"That's their prerogative," he muttered resignedly.

"I'll be headed off now," Dayna said.

"Okay. Thanks for everything. Have a good day."

"You, too."

A few minutes later, Gene went downstairs and mingled with some of his guests. He hated to see them leave, as they were almost like family now that he was all alone as a man and host. Though it wasn't his choice, he accepted it. But that didn't mean he had no interest in having someone special in his life. Sloane was a good choice, were it to turn out that way. She definitely seemed to have herself together as a business lady and was a lovely, sensually appealing woman.

He'd enjoyed having lunch with Sloane, gazing into those eyes with their depths of intriguing darkness. Even watching the way her lips moved while eating or drinking drove Gene crazy with desire. What he wouldn't give to see that mouth in action on him.

Gene suppressed his libido, turning his attention to the luau that was sure to put on a show for Sloane and give him an opportunity to see her when they were both out of their element.

Sloane marveled at the sights as she sat in the passenger seat of Gene's Subaru Outback. They had just passed through Kihei with its multitude of small shops and stores and were now in Lahaina, an nineteenth-century whaling port, with swaying coconut palm trees, timber-frame buildings and breathtaking views of the West Maui Mountains as the setting sun cast an enchanting glow on them.

She turned to Gene's handsome profile as he spoke about Maui and its districts as if he'd grown up there. His head was freshly shaven and his dimpled cheek was pronounced.

"We actually thought about buying a house in Lahaina to convert into the bed-and-breakfast," he was saying, "but in the end, we got a better deal and location in Wailea."

"I think you made the right choice." Sloane couldn't imagine him being anywhere else in Maui.

He faced her with a sexy smile. "I think so, too."

Sloane felt a tingling sensation at the carnal tone of his words. She suspected that had been his intent and she fell for it, unable to help herself. "How long did it take you to get a handle on the island and its many areas and activities?" she asked, switching her thoughts to a safer topic.

"Not very long. You can get a feel for everything pretty quickly once you settle in. Besides, with the B&B I had little choice but to get to know the surroundings as quickly as possible so I'd be equipped to respond to visitors and would-be guests and their range of questions about Maui."

"Makes sense," Sloane said. "I'm still trying to get to know the island and all of its secrets and treasures."

"You'll know it backward and forward in no time flat," Gene told her encouragingly.

"How can you be so sure?" she asked curiously.

He smiled. "You didn't get to be director of guest relations at a major resort hotel in Hawaii without having the intrinsic tools to make it work."

"Good answer." He was also good for her ego. Not that she had low self-esteem, but it was nice to get such positive feedback.

"It's also the truth," Gene assured her. "But if you ever need a little help getting around or discovering interesting little places or hideaways that you can impart to your guests, don't hesitate to ask."

"I'll keep that in mind," Sloane said appreciatively. "I'm sure I will take you up on that sooner or later."

"I hope so."

Soon they arrived in Kaanapali, formerly part of a sugar plantation that was now transformed into a world-class luxury resort area lined with high-end hotels and condominiums, meandering golf courses, sandy white beaches and stunning sunset views of the island of Lanai. Kaanapali Beach, along a stretch of rugged lava coastline, was divided by a 300-foot extinct volcano called Black Rock.

Sloane and Gene were greeted at the Kaanapali Beach luau with a shell lei before being served mai tais and touring the luau grounds. There were local artisans and their crafts on display and traditional Hawaiian music in the air. But what really piqued Sloane's interest was checking out the imu pit, an underground barbecue pit where a whole pig was being roasted.

"That's fascinating," she said a little squeamishly. "I feel sorry for the pig, though."

Gene chuckled. "Don't worry. It has no idea of the spectacle it's making. Not to mention how tasty it will be when served."

Sloane tried not to think about the process so much as the end result. They watched as the luau emcee announced the uncovering of the imu pit, indicating that dinner was nearly ready to be served.

"Help yourself," Gene said a few minutes later as they moved along the buffet line, loaded with a variety of dishes.

"I'm not sure where to start," Sloane told him, her eyes darting to the many foods and desserts. She wished she had starved herself for a day to be able to eat more than she intended to without putting on any pounds.

"My advice is to try a little bit of everything that captures your fancy. And don't be afraid to put yourself out there and try something new."

Sloane laughed. "Easy for you to say, but I have to use some restraint and watch my figure."

Gene gave her the once-over. "I wouldn't worry about that. From what I can see, your figure is perfect. Whatever you eat tonight isn't likely to tarnish that one bit for someone who works out regularly like you do."

"You're probably right," she acquiesced. *Does he really think my figure is perfect?*

She decided to go for it and try the lomi lomi salmon, Polynesian banana, sea-bean duck salad, mango-sauce poi, and a couple of slices of kalua pork. Finding everything utterly delicious but feeling guilty nonetheless, Sloane promised herself she would put in a couple of extra running miles tomorrow to make up for it.

She watched, amused, as Gene devoured fishcake with mussels, steamed jasmine rice, Kula greens salad and a generous portion of the kalua pork. They both had the chocolate macadamia-nut cream pie for dessert.

Afterward, they focused their attention on the spectacular Maui luau show, which featured pulsating music and synchronized drumbeats. Beautiful, curvy island girls moved their hips gracefully in sensual dancing with Hawaiian, Maori, Samoan and other Tahitian influences, while hunky male hula dancers performed choreographed, athletic dance moves without missing a beat.

After that came the Samoan fire knife dance. Sloane was thoroughly captivated as daring young men twirled knives of fire, passing them skillfully among one another. One member actually flawlessly performed a double fire knife dance, causing the audience to gasp from time to time.

"Hope he knows what he's doing," Gene whispered in her ear as the fire came perilously close to burning the dancer.

"So do I," seconded Sloane, holding her breath till the routine came to a successful conclusion.

All the dancers came back onstage for a final body-shaking, feet-moving, dazzling display with high-octane music matching them every step of the way before the luau ended.

"Wow," Sloane said with a chuckle as she eyed Gene. "That was amazing."

"Yes, it was," he agreed. "They really know their stuff."

"It certainly kept my attention. Thanks for inviting me."

Gene put his hand across hers on the table. "I'm glad you came. I wanted you to see what a true luau was all about—taking nothing away from the one at the Island Shores, of course."

"We could definitely learn a thing or two," Sloane admitted. "I'll have to talk to my boss about that."

"We can all learn something new," Gene said, peering at her deeply. "The real question is whether or not that knowledge is put to good use."

Sloane felt the heat of their skin still touching. She could only imagine just how high the temperature would rise if those sure hands were all over her body. She met Gene's gaze, which was just as searing.

"I guess only time will tell," she told him, reading ardently between the lines.

Gene drove Sloane back to the hotel, wishing instead that they were going to his place, where things could be taken in a different direction. Making love to Sloane had been practically all that occupied his mind from the time the female hula dancers were strutting their stuff till now. Gene envisioned Sloane on stage giving him a very sexy, sensual private hula dance, until neither of them could hold back any longer and had to have each other. But he didn't want to jump the gun on what seemed to be strong vibes between them, even if they weren't quite ready to get into anything that suggested a committed relationship. Besides, something told him that waiting for the right time for nature to take its course would more than pay off in the long run. He would see to that.

"Have you visited the other islands?" Sloane broke the brief silence.

"Every one of them except Molokai and Niihau," Gene replied. "And I expect to get to those sooner or later."

"So you're really into this island thing, huh?"

He grinned crookedly. "You could say that. Ever since my first visit to Hawaii—Honolulu—with my mother and stepfather back in the day, I've always had a fascination with the islands. Now one of the islands is home for me."

"For both of us," Sloane added.

Gene liked the sound of that. "So you're planning on sticking around for a while then?"

"Yes, at this point. It's still early in my move to Maui, but I expect the job to keep me here for some time. I'd love to acclimate myself to Maui like you have. Besides, I hate to move if I can help it."

"I hear you. Packing up and unpacking can be a drag."

Sloane faced him. "Does that mean you'd never consider moving back to the mainland?"

Gene paused contemplatively. "Not at all," he said. "If there is a good enough reason for me to return to the mainland, I'd be happy to."

"Maybe there will be someday," she hinted. "You just never know."

Gene could well imagine moving back to the continental United States for someone as compelling and beautiful as Sloane. Even if marrying again seemed like a long shot—and he was pretty sure Sloane was just as opposed to it at this time in her life—it didn't mean there couldn't be a compromise in building a steady relationship if both parties were on the same wavelength.

"I agree," he told her. "Keeping an open mind makes anything possible."

She sighed. "I'm afraid that some things in life are set in stone."

Gene cocked a brow over the steering wheel. "You mean death and taxes," he half joked.

"Yes, that and keeping an eye on one's priorities in life," Sloane said.

He forced a chuckle. "Spoken like a true business-woman."

"I'm not all business," Sloane said defensively.

Gene considered that they had just cozied up together at a luau. Then there was that sweet kiss. "I can see that."

"All right. Just wanted to be sure."

He met her eyes. "I am sure. You're willing to let your hair down for a good time. I commend you there."

"I guess I should commend you back for being willing to step outside of your box too from time to time," she told him.

Gene couldn't deny the obvious symmetry. "Looks as though we have something in common."

Sloane laughed. "Just one thing?"

Gene cracked a smile. "How about a few things?"

"That sounds better."

It did to him as well, giving them something to build upon.

He pulled up to the Island Shores, wondering if Sloane would invite him up for a nightcap.

"Thank you for a nice evening," she told him.

"It was only nice because you were there," he said truthfully.

"I'm not sure about that."

"I am. Those hula dancers can't hold a candle to you," Gene assured her.

"I could say the same thing about the male dancers," Sloane said.

Gene took that as his cue to make a move. He leaned over and moved toward Sloane's alluring mouth, staring into her delicious dark eyes. When she showed no desire to stop him, he kissed those luscious lips. Sloane opened her mouth, allowing him to slip his tongue inside. His tongue danced with hers as they circled one another's desirously. He could taste the remnants of Sloane's mai tai, turning him on even more and heightening his desire.

Sloane sucked greedily on his lower lip as Gene sucked her upper lip appetizingly while the sexual sounds reverberated in his ears. Gene loved kissing and being kissed by Sloane. His erection pounded against his trousers, begging to come out and make its way deep inside her. Fighting the urge, Gene kept his focus and enjoyment on the moment at hand as their kissing picked up in its intensity.

Sloane's tongue whipped in and out of his mouth, teasing and tasting him while Gene pressed his lips to hers tightly in a feverish kiss that left him breathless yet wanting so much more. Sloane wrapped her hands around his head, opening her mouth wider and drawing him in with utter abandon.

They were both panting and the temperature rose to a dangerously high level in the car as Gene nibbled on the inside of Sloane's lip, wanting to experience every piece of her kiss. He put his tongue between her lips again, enjoying more of what she offered to him as a man hungry for passion with a lovely and immensely sexual woman.

He brought one hand up to her breast, reveling in the fullness and feel of it. His finger fell across her hard nipple and Sloane jerked. Gene gripped her entire breast through her blouse, caressing joyously before stroking Sloane's nipple up, down and sideways. Her breathing quickened and she bit into his lip, causing Gene to wince.

The kiss continued unabated for several minutes, and Gene became lost in Sloane and her swollen lips. After she gave him a final powerful smooch, she pulled back, releasing his head from her firm grip.

"Getting a bit toasty in here," she murmured with a long sigh.

"No complaints here," Gene said, coming back down to earth.

"Or here. You're a terrific kisser, which I believe was already established a couple of days ago."

"Takes one to know one," he uttered, licking his lips and tasting hers.

"I'm glad you feel that way." Sloane ran two fingers across her mouth. "As much as I'd love to go further, I think we'd better leave it here tonight."

A slice of disappointment crossed Gene's face, but he quickly overcame it, exercising patience. "Probably a good idea."

She smiled. "I'll see you later."

"When?" Gene pressed, hating to think that later could be longer than he could manage to stay away from her.

Sloane paused and took out her cell phone. "What's your number?"

He gave it to her, taking the opportunity to add Sloane's number to his cell phone.

"We'll be speaking soon," she said.

"That a promise?"

She grinned. "Yes, it's definitely a promise, especially now that we're both just a phone call away."

"Do you want me to walk you up?" Gene thought to ask. *And maybe stay for a while.*

"That won't be necessary, but thanks for the offer."

Before getting out of the car, Sloane gave him another stirring kiss that Gene felt all over.

"Good night, Gene."

"Good night."

He watched briefly as she approached the well-lit hotel before driving off, the kiss very much on his mind, as well as the lady herself.

Chapter 4

The next morning, Sloane was awakened by her cell phone chiming. After dreaming about Gene and the potent kiss that left her nerve endings tingling, she thought it might be him telling her he'd had the same dream.

When she dragged herself out of bed and grabbed the phone, Sloane saw from the caller ID that it was Gail Littleton, her good friend from Raleigh.

"Hey, girl," Gail spoke spiritedly. "Hope I didn't wake you up?"

"You didn't," Sloane lied. She needed to get up anyhow.

"I wanted to check in with you to see how things are going in gorgeous Maui."

"Just fabulous so far," Sloane said.

"Darn, I was afraid you'd say that." Gail chuckled. "Please tell me you miss Raleigh at least a little bit."

"I do—a little," Sloane didn't mind saying. "I miss my friends like you and the sense of familiarity. But…"

"But Hawaii is…well, Hawaii."

Sloane smiled. "You took the words right out of my mouth. With the perfect weather and beautiful setting, what more could a person ask for?"

"How about a man?" Gail spoke bluntly. "Of course, I'm sure there is no shortage of fine-looking, fit men roaming the beaches in skimpy swimsuits."

"You know I'm here to work," Sloane said as if to convince herself.

"So work. That doesn't mean there's no time for play with the right playmate. Or have you sworn off men for good these days?"

Sloane mused about Gene's kiss, which had seared her soul. And when he'd stimulated her nipple, she'd nearly screamed, it felt so good.

"No, I haven't sworn off men," she told her. "As a matter of fact, I am talking to one guy…" And maybe a bit more than talking.

"Mmm—" hummed Gail.

"Nothing serious. We're both busy individuals, but found time to spend together. It's still early though."

"What does he do for a living?"

"He owns a bed-and-breakfast," Sloane answered.

"Interesting." Gail took a breath. "Maybe I'll stay there whenever I can save up enough money to fly to Hawaii."

"Great. I'm sure he'll be happy to have you as a guest."

They spoke for a few more minutes before Sloane gracefully cut short the conversation. "I have to do my daily run," she told her. "I'll talk to you soon."

"Count on it," Gail said.

Sloane washed her face and threw on running attire. She was out the door and on the beach in no time flat.

When she passed by Malloy's Bed and Breakfast, Sloane wondered if Gene was a runner. He was obviously in tiptop shape, but maybe he got that way through lifting weights or swimming. Or did his conditioning come naturally?

She thought about detouring to visit him, but decided it was best to keep up with her routine and give the man a little breathing room. Even if Gene Malloy and his expertise as a kisser was very much on Sloane's mind. Along with, she suspected, his strong skills in the bedroom.

In the afternoon, Sloane met with a rental agent to look at a Wailea condominium, her second one of the day. It was a one-bedroom, fully furnished, air-conditioned unit on the sixth floor in a gated community. The condo was on the beach and walking distance from the Island Shores Resort. All in all, it seemed like the perfect place for Sloane.

"The condo was recently renovated," the rental agent, Betty, told Sloane as they toured it. "The rent includes free cable TV and high-speed internet."

"Those are definite plusses," Sloane said, though she rarely had time to watch TV. Being able to work from home online seamlessly was certainly a good thing.

"Most of our renters agree with you there." Betty opened the vertical blinds in the small living room. "All your utilities are also included in the rent, along with a state-of-the-art security system. It's doubtful you'll ever need the latter, as this is a very safe area."

Sloane smiled. "It's sounding better all the time." She took in the furnishings, which were casual and neatly arranged, blending in well with the lighter shade of gray walls. There was a ceiling fan overhead.

Betty turned on the kitchen light. "Everything you need to produce some authentic Hawaiian dishes is at your disposal."

"I can see that." Sloane glanced at the new stainless-steel appliances and granite countertops. She imagined cooking Gene a scrumptious meal, even if it would take a while to get the Hawaiian cuisine down pat.

They went to the bedroom. It was small, but large enough for a single woman to get around in comfortably. Sloane liked the rustic log furniture, including an Adirondack bed, bamboo grommet panels and valence window treatment, along with a ceiling fan.

Sloane was shown the beautifully manicured grounds and flower garden on the premises before they went back inside.

"So what do you think?" Betty asked anxiously.

"I love it," declared Sloane, more than ready to have a place—this one—of her own.

The rental agent beamed. "Then let's get you into this unit and it's yours to enjoy."

"Sounds like a great idea!"

Sloane filled out the necessary paperwork, knowing that her references were impeccable and a nice-paying job ensured that she could afford the luxury condo. Someday she wanted something with a greater sense of permanence and attachment to hang her hat. But for now, this was more than enough to make her feel right at home in Maui.

The phone was ringing off the hook this morning with calls coming in from as far away as Australia and as near as Oahu. Gene was glad that Dayna was on hand today to handle most of them. He was aware that in many instances callers were merely inquiring and comparison shopping. Some opted for the traditional hotel, while others sought something farther away from the water or less cozy. Gene was cool with that. He understood it was a competitive environment and only wanted to get his fair share of business while continuing to attract new guests and repeat visitors.

Standing in his private suite, Gene looked at his cell phone, hoping Sloane might call. There was no message. She had promised to ring him soon for their next get-together. But maybe the following day was too soon for her, if not him. He had a mind to call her and tell her he was thinking about her, especially that kiss that had rocked his foundation and left him wanting her in the worst way.

Maybe that wasn't such a good idea. He didn't want to crowd the beautiful lady, scaring her off. While the thought of Sloane caused Gene's stomach to tie up in knots, he had to respect that she had other things on her mind right now than him. Whether or not he would ever move to the top of the list remained to be seen.

When his cell phone rang, Gene's heart skipped a beat. He saw that the caller was Walter Griffin, his best friend from Detroit.

"What's up, man?" Walter asked routinely.

"I'm good." Gene stepped by the window, which gave him a bird's-eye view of the sea and sand. "How are you?"

"Same old, same old. The job brings in a paycheck and the wife is still keeping me up late into the night."

Gene smiled. Walter was a law professor and his wife, Talia, a high school teacher. They had been married for nearly ten years and neither seemed to be able to get enough of the other.

"The job aside, lucky you, Talia keeps the fires burning," Gene told him enviously, and couldn't help but consider Sloane keeping him up making love into the wee hours of the morning.

"Oh, yes, on fire all the time," Walter said with a chuckle.

"And have you landed one of those Hawaii mermaids yet?"

"Not exactly," Gene responded thoughtfully. "But I'm working on it."

"Cool. No reason to go it alone."

"I know. That won't be the case forever. Right now the B&B keeps me going."

Walter paused. "I run into Lynda every now and then."

"Good for you," Gene muttered with regard to his ex-wife.

"She's been seeing a local city councilman."

"I'm happy for her."

"Really?"

"Why not?" Gene said defensively. "We've been divorced for two years. What she does with her life now is her own business."

"Yeah, I guess," Walter said. "Anyway, the main reason I'm calling, other than to catch up, is that Talia's been bugging me to take her to Hawaii ever since, well, you decided to go into business there. So I've finally given in and thought maybe we should take a week in Maui to celebrate our anniversary."

"That's sounds fabulous. What a way to celebrate the occasion."

"Of course, we'd want to stay at your bed-and-breakfast."

"You are more than welcome," Gene told him, making a mental note to keep a room open. "It would be great to see Talia again, too."

"I was hoping you'd be open to it." Walter took a breath. "I didn't want things to be awkward with Lynda out of the picture."

"They won't be," Gene assured him. "I've moved on since then." If he played his cards right, Sloane just might command all of his attention in the romance-and-passion department.

"All right. I'll let Talia know that her dream is about to come true. Who knows, maybe we'll even renew our vows while we're out there."

"What a wonderful idea. I'll be happy to help set that up for you."

After the call, Gene got back to playing host for his current guests, even if his mind was still very much on Sloane and the sexual chemistry between them that was so red-hot he knew it was only a matter of time before it exploded into some dynamic sex.

Kendra was the first person Sloane told about her new condo, sharing the news over lunch that afternoon.

"Sounds like you found the perfect place," Kendra said.

"I think so, for the time being." Sloane forked some of her Caesar salad. "At least I won't have to live out of a hotel room, albeit a very nice one."

"I'm jealous already," Kendra teased. "The only ocean view in my house is a picture hanging in my living room."

Sloane laughed. "You can come by whenever you like and see the ocean or whatever," she offered, hoping she wouldn't abuse the privilege.

"How sweet. I'll keep that in mind." Kendra dabbed a napkin to her lips. "I suppose now that you've got your own place, things will really heat up between you and Gene."

"Maybe," Sloane said, as she could hardly think of anything else. "First, I'd like to invite him over for dinner and see where things go from there."

"Well, you know what they say about food being the key to a man's heart and all that."

"I'm not exactly reaching out for his heart," Sloane said with a playful grin. "At the moment, I'm much more interested in other parts of his anatomy."

Kendra chuckled. "You're so bad."

Sloane colored. "Just being honest. Neither of us is looking for love so much as lust and friendship. It's easier that way, and no one gets hurt."

"In my experience there's a fine line between love, lust and friendship."

"It's a line I'd rather not cross while I get where I want to with my career," Sloane told her.

"Do you think you can really differentiate your feelings so easily?"

"Why not? I have so far." Sloane had to admit that she had never before met anyone like Gene, whose powerful, manly presence and damned good looks made her at least have second thoughts about her long-held rules. In the end, she wanted to remain steadfast, so neither of them ended up regretting whatever they seemed on the verge of starting.

"Hope it works out the way you want," Kendra said.

"Me, too." Sloane lifted her glass. "First things first. I'll see if Gene is agreeable to dinner and whatever else may end up on the menu."

At 8:00 p.m., after spending hours getting situated in her new home, Sloane called Gene. She was uncharacteristically nervous as his phone rang, as if he had given her any reason to be. She sucked in a deep breath, hoping she wouldn't have to leave a message, preferring to actually talk to him.

"Hello, there," Gene answered, his smooth voice deep and sexy.

Sloane folded her legs beneath her in the chair. "Hi. Are you busy?"

"Not really. Just hanging around the house socializing with my guests, sometimes playing babysitter, other times referee."

"Does it ever get old, not being able to separate your personal and professional life?" Sloane asked curiously as she wondered if she could do the same.

"Actually, it's just the opposite," he claimed. "Running a bed-and-breakfast, each day brings about new adventures and sometimes challenges, with a constant changeover of guests. Everyone has a story and they're only too happy to share it with the others. It's almost like being at summer camp where the campers are essentially one big happy family."

"I never went to camp," Sloane admitted, but almost wished she had. Especially if he'd been one of the campers. "But I see your point."

"Thought you would." Gene paused. "So how did your house search go?"

"Better than expected. I found a nice beachfront condo."

"Great! Congratulations."

"Thanks." Sloane stilled her nerves. "If you're not busy, I'd like to invite you over for dinner tomorrow night."

Gene didn't hesitate. "I'd love to have dinner with you at your new place…on one condition."

"Which is?"

"You let me bring the wine."

She brightened. "You're on."

"Then it's a date," Gene said sweetly.

"How does seven-thirty sound?"

"Like music to my ears. I'll be there."

"Wonderful," Sloane told him. "Hope you still like good old-fashioned continental U.S. dishes?"

"Of course," he assured her. "Feel free to make whatever you're good at and I'll be only too happy to eat it."

Sloan laughed. "Sounds like a can't-lose proposition."

"Maybe because that's what it is," Gene spoke confidently. "We're both on the winning team here. All we need to do is play the game."

"I see."

Sloane thought the metaphors were cute. Were they really embarking on a game—perhaps of truth or dare? Or engaging in something with much more substance? She gave him her address, which was only a few blocks away from his bed-and-breakfast. Sloane could imagine that with the short distance, they could easily go back and forth if this were the direction their burgeoning friendship was headed.

Ever since talking to Sloane on the phone, Gene had been looking forward to going to her new condo for dinner. It was a great way to get to know each other better in a more intimate setting than a luau, hotel café, or even a bed-and-breakfast with people steadily coming and going and private time a luxury. He was convinced that the electricity generated from their kisses deserved to be explored in depth. Gene strongly suspected that Sloane felt the same way, even if she wasn't looking for marriage or even a long-term commitment. He was more than willing to let things play out and go from there.

Wanting to make a good impression, he decided to go dressier than his normal casual attire, wearing a tan sport coat over a designer black T-shirt and light brown twill slacks. He replaced his usual slip-ons or exercise shoes with leather loafers and sprayed on his favorite cologne.

Gene was a few minutes early as he rang the bell. He

hoped Sloane didn't have a problem with that. Maybe he could even give her a hand with the food.

When the door opened, Gene was floored by the exquisite vision before him. Sloane was wearing a satin halter tiered black dress with a generous amount of cleavage showing and black sandals. Her hair was appealingly loose and hung evenly across her shoulders.

It took Gene a moment to get his mouth to speak. "Hey," he managed.

"Well, hello," she said, flashing white teeth through alluring lips. "Welcome to my new home."

"Thanks for inviting me." He scanned her body, then settled on Sloane's lovely face. "You look beautiful tonight."

"Why, thank you." She beamed. "You're looking pretty spiffy yourself."

Gene's cheeks dimpled. "I didn't want to underdress."

"You didn't. Please come in."

He stepped into the foyer and immediately got a sense of warmth and belonging. The place was small by the standards of his bed-and-breakfast, but neat and organized, as well as a great location.

"I brought this." Gene handed Sloane the bottle. "It's a pineapple-and-passion-fruit white wine straight from the Maui Winery at Ulupalakua Ranch."

"Hmm, sounds tasty," said Sloane. "Can't wait to try it out."

"Do you need help with anything?"

She met his eyes. "You can pour the wine if you like."

"It would be my pleasure to do so," he told her.

They went to the kitchen, where Gene's nostrils picked up more heavily the scent of food. It made his stomach growl, but not half as much as the way Sloane turned him on in that sexy dress.

"The wine goblets are in that cabinet," Sloane pointed above the dishwasher. "I'm still trying to learn my way around here and what came with the place."

"Perfectly understandable." Gene found the goblets. He put them on the counter and opened the wine. "Even after four years, I'm still sometimes totally in the dark at the B&B when it comes to where some things are stored."

Sloane looked at him as she stood over the stove. "I guess it helps keep you on your toes."

"Yeah, I suppose." He poured wine into one of the glasses and walked over to her. "Try it and tell me what you think."

She put the glass to her mouth and sipped. "Um, very tasty."

Gene smiled contentedly. "I think so, too. It's certainly quite different from the norm."

"I agree." The tip of Sloane's tongue slipped out onto her lower lip.

"So what's for dinner?" Gene glanced over her shoulder. He could see that there was chicken gravy in one pot and what looked like greens in another. And whatever she had in the oven smelled delicious.

"Oh, just a little something I've put together," she stated mysteriously. "Hope you like."

He looked at her with an admiring gaze. "Yes, I like very much."

Sloane flushed. "Other than me."

"From where I stand," Gene said ardently, "there is no one other than you."

Sloane tried not to be swept under by Gene's steady and decidedly provocative gaze, persuasive charms and handsome features. At least not till they finished the meal she had spent two hours preparing. It consisted of baked lemon chicken, mashed sweet potatoes, mustard greens, biscuits and old-fashioned gravy she'd learned how to make from her mother.

After everything was set on the dining room table, Sloane joined Gene there. She wanted very much to kiss him again and be kissed by him the way he'd kissed her the other night. She chose patience and the near certainty that the strong sexual pull between them would manifest itself soon enough.

"This looks delicious," remarked Gene, scooping up mashed sweet potatoes.

"Wait until you taste before telling me what you think," Sloane told him, though fairly confident she had hit the right notes on the meal.

"Fair enough." He sampled a bit of everything and then broke into a grin. "Everything is great. I'd say you've sold me on your ability to cook."

She produced a generous smile while wondering what else she could sell him. "I wanted the first meal cooked in my condo to be special."

"It is, and so is the cook."

"My ego just might explode if you keep that up."

Gene chuckled. "What—can't a man tell a woman what he thinks of her?"

"As often as you like," she answered playfully. "As long as I'm free to dish out compliments in return."

"You've got my permission," he said, grabbing a biscuit. "But maybe you'd better hold off on that till you taste one of my meals. Or see how else I might earn those accolades…."

Sloane felt a tingle between her legs as she considered his earning such accolades in bed. Would she ever be able to keep up with him? She ate some of the food, though her appetite had swung in the direction of sexual satisfaction.

"If you say so," she spoke, turned on by the insinuation.

He laughed. "I like your style."

"I like yours too."

"Good thing that sneaker wave came when it did. Otherwise I might never have gotten the chance to dive into those pools of nighttime eyes staring back at me."

"Guess we both have something to be thankful for," Sloane said boldly.

"Amen to that." Gene lifted his glass and she followed suit.

"Why don't we take these into the living room?" Sloane realized both had eaten as much as they cared to and should be in a more comfortable setting.

"Yes, why don't we."

They sat on the sofa. Sloane knew she had Gene's full attention, as he had hers. She wasn't about to let the evening pass without allowing the smoldering chemistry between them to play out as it should.

"This is certainly a beautiful island," she murmured.

"Not half as beautiful as you," Gene countered, taking her in with a look of desire.

Sloane loved the compliment but sought to downplay it. "Me versus Maui…hmm…not so sure I'm the winner."

"Trust me when I say you are. Sun, sand and waves are nice, don't get me wrong, that's why I'm here. But they're no match for a gorgeous, beguiling, sexy woman like yourself."

Sloane was getting warmer by the second. "You're pretty hot too," she said. "I'm sure you're told that all the time."

"Maybe not all the time, but enough." His gaze on her

face was unblinking. "Doesn't mean as much, though, as when it comes from someone I've got my eye on."

She absorbed the intensity of his stare. "So you're really interested in me?"

"Didn't that kiss make it pretty clear?" Gene asked.

"It told me that you enjoy kissing," Sloan teased. "So do I."

He lifted his glass. "It seems like we're going around in circles here."

Her lashes fluttered innocently. "Oh, you think so, do you?"

"What I think is that you are driving me absolutely wild in that sexy-as-hell dress."

"Am I?"

"How could you not?" Gene voiced thickly. "Especially when I've wanted to take it off you from the moment I walked in the door."

"Was anything stopping you?" Sloane dared ask.

"Only sheer willpower that's melting by the second."

She sipped more wine. "So let it melt away."

Gene took her glass and put it on the table. "Say no more," he uttered, sliding a smooth hand across her cheek.

Sloane readied herself as Gene leaned over and pressed his mouth into hers passionately and with the same confidence and expertise he'd shown previously. Only this time there was clearly a greater sense of urgency, as though he wanted to rip her clothes off and take her without missing a beat.

Matching this wanton desire to have him inside her, Sloane jumped right into the kiss, opening her mouth wide and making him do the same. She sucked on his hard lips, loving the taste of wine on them, and put her tongue inside Gene's mouth, searching it for every bit of joy the kiss could bring. In turn, his tongue went into her mouth and Sloane was tickled sexually as Gene used it to kiss her in new and exciting ways.

As his body pressed into her, Sloane felt Gene's mighty erection screaming to be released from his trousers and driven inside her. The thought that he wanted her so badly turned Sloane on even more. She ran her hands up and down his back, intoxicated by his manly scent heightened by his seductive cologne.

Gene put his hand beneath her dress and between her legs. Sloane wasn't wearing any underwear. She nearly climaxed on the spot when his fingers touched and teased her, making her wetter and more desirous to make love to him than she'd already been. She chewed on his upper lip, caught in the fever of wanting this man more than she could imagine.

Seeming unfazed by her sure indication of needing much more from him, Gene coolly continued to stroke between Sloane's legs in slow, sheer torture while never removing his mouth from hers, and the kiss left Sloane weak and essentially a prisoner to their intimacy. She breathed in deeply, yielding to the potency of kissing Gene and his fingers caressing her with the deliberation of a man who knew exactly what he was doing and wouldn't be denied.

When Sloane could no longer hold back, she had an orgasm right then and there, as his fiery kiss and nimble fingers brought her to new heights. Her pulse raced and body quivered almost uncontrollably till the sexual urge had reached its peak. But instead of feeling satisfied, Sloane realized it only made her hungrier for Gene and what he could give her. She suspected this had been his mission all along.

She unlocked their lips and gazed directly at him while

barely catching her breath. "I think we'd better take this to the bedroom."

Gene regarded her with ravenous eyes. "I doubt that anything on earth could stop us from doing just that."

He got to his feet and effortlessly lifted Sloane into his arms. She wrapped her arms around his neck and quivered with anticipation at what was to come next.

Chapter 5

Gene tore his lips away from Sloane as he put her gently on the bed. He stood tall as she looked up at him with desperate eyes, wanting him inside her as much as he did. He knew she'd already had an orgasm from his deft touch and powerful kisses. This pleased him as much for the way it intensified his sexual desire for her as giving Sloane a quick fix before it was his turn to release the pent-up cravings she instilled in him.

When Sloane started to remove her dress, Gene spoke out, "Don't. Leave it on. I want to make love to you the first time while you're wearing that very sexy dress."

"If that's what you want," she cooed.

"No, it's you that I want," he corrected. "And now I intend to have you."

Stripping off his own clothes in full view of her, Gene wanted Sloane to see all she was getting of him, confident she would like everything she saw. He grabbed a packet from his pants, removed the condom and slid it across his full erection.

He climbed onto the bed, half atop Sloane. Her skin was soft as cotton and her body moist and inviting. Forcing himself to use willpower, Gene held off from entering her just yet, wanting to taste Sloane's sex first. He moved down her and put his head beneath her dress. Her womanly scent thoroughly captivated him, making him mad with lust.

Gene kissed her sweet spot, feeling a slight tremor from Sloane. She was very wet, needing him. He flicked his tongue across her clitoris, enjoying the pleasure he gave her. He licked her a few more times, fighting his own powerful urge. Now it was time they came together this night.

Gene came out from beneath her dress and peered lasciviously at Sloane. She stared back at him hotly.

"Make love to me," she demanded, breathing heavily.

"With pleasure," he promised lustfully.

Sandwiching himself between her spread legs, Gene guided himself into Sloane's vagina and moved in deeply. She was tight and fluid around him, bringing about great satisfaction as he thrust in and out, watching her beautiful face. Her eyes were closed and mouth open slightly. He bent down and took those juicy lips, kissing her with a renewed appetite.

Sloane wrapped her legs around Gene's back and held on to his shoulders tightly as the sex heated up. He loved the feel of being wedged inside her, their bodies locked in coitus. The urge to release himself was more powerful than anything Gene could remember. It was time to let go.

He cupped Sloane's buttocks and dove farther inside her, groaning as she constricted around him. Sloane sighed hotly into his mouth. Gene's lips covered her with a continuous kiss while his orgasm consumed him and his heart pounded with satisfaction.

Even after he had reached the height of ecstasy, Gene did not let up in making love to Sloane till her body sizzled with another climax. The bed shook beneath them as they rode the wave together before slowly descending, kissing their way back down to earth.

Gene gave Sloane one final kiss before pulling out of her. "You were incredible," he said, knowing that was an understatement.

"Look who's talking," she countered, her breath hot on his face.

A grin curved one side of his mouth. "So we were both amazing—together."

"Yes, we were."

"That was one hell of a dessert."

She flashed her teeth sexily. "Good thing you left a little room after dinner."

"Saved the best for last," Gene declared.

"So I'm the best, huh?" Sloane looked at him beneath fluttering lashes.

"Absolutely!" He kissed her again. "Or haven't I convinced you enough?"

"What if I said no?" Her eyes grew seductively. "Do you have anything left in you?"

Gene chuckled. "Is that a challenge?"

"You tell me," Sloane tossed back audaciously.

She was so enticing that Gene became aroused again. Besides, he was up for a dare, especially when Sloane was offering herself as the grand prize. It was a prize he wouldn't let slip away. Not this night, anyway.

"Oh, I'm just getting started," he spoke with yearning. "Or should I say we are—"

The next day, Sloane was back at work. She was a bit tired from the sexual workout that had lasted well into the night, but chipper nonetheless. And satiated from Gene's sexual prowess, which was every bit her match. She wasn't sure where things were going with Gene, if anywhere, only that she was happy to have him in her life right now for what they gave each other. He certainly seemed to have no complaints, making for a good understanding between them.

After she made her rounds through the hotel, making sure guests had what they needed and setting into motion any requests made, Sloane met with the general manager, Alan Komoda, in his office.

"Hello, Sloane," he said politely. "Have a seat."

Sloane sat in one of the plush chairs across from his desk, wondering what was going on. Had someone complained about how she was doing her job? Or was there another, more ominous reason for summoning her?

"I heard that you found yourself a place to live," Alan said. "Do you like it?"

"Yes, it's nice." Sloane resisted the inclination to slouch.

"Good." He paused, making her feel slightly uneasy. "Well, I just wanted to let you know that I'm very pleased with the job you've done thus far."

She breathed a sigh of relief. "Thank you."

"No, thank you. I respect the professionalism you have shown and your enthusiasm for the job. I can't say that about all the people who have come to work for us."

"I appreciate the confidence you have in me," Sloane told him. "I love this hotel and want to do my best to make our guests feel right at home."

"I think you're doing just that," Alan told her. "The group from Japan we had in last week couldn't say enough about how you were available to assist them in every way to make their trip a big success."

Sloane smiled brightly, remembering them. "I'm so glad to hear they had a good time."

"Anyway, I wanted to commend you personally for taking the bull by the horns and stepping right into your role without missing a step." He leaned forward. "I'll let you get back to work now."

Sloane left the office, feeling good about how things were shaping up in her life. Her job had always been the most important thing in her world, and Alan's praise seemed to justify that. But Gene was a delight in her personal life that she hadn't seen coming. Having a male friend with incredible benefits in the bedroom was certainly worthwhile and something to continue enjoying as long as he felt the same.

Caught in thought, Sloane had barely been cognizant of the elevator stopping till the doors opened. Kendra stepped in, a huge smile on her face.

"What's got you so bubbly?" Sloane asked.

"I've just been asked out on a date," she gushed.

"Oh…?" Sloane regarded her.

"Yes. He's a member of the band that plays in our club. He's so cute."

"You go, girl," Sloane said with a chuckle.

"I intend to—as far as I can." Kendra giggled. "Speaking of…how did the dinner date go with Gene?"

Sloane smiled, reflecting on it. "About as good as could be expected."

"Really, that good?"

"Even better," Sloane admitted.

"In other words, you took him to bed?" Kendra asked bluntly.

"I'd say it's more we took each other to bed." Sloane mused about the incredible sex that rocked her world. "It was wonderful."

"I guess it was, judging by the glow on your face."

Sloane blushed. "Don't get the wrong idea."

Kendra's mouth twisted. "Which is?"

"We're not in love or anything," she stated, as if needing to clarify. "We just…"

"Hooked up," Kendra said. "I get it. You don't have to be in love to be deeply in lust. Not in Maui, anyway. Just let it happen and have fun."

"I intend to," Sloane promised. "And I could say the same to you."

The doors opened and the two stepped out into the lobby, where Sloane returned her focus to the job at hand, even if Gene Malloy was never too far from her mind.

"Someone's in a good mood this afternoon," Ngozi said when she saw Gene sitting in the living room.

He grinned, not too surprised that it showed. "I'm always in a good mood," he said, trying to downplay it. "Must be that infectious Hawaii atmosphere."

Ngozi smiled. "That certainly helps. I'm definitely going to miss it and everything else about this place."

Gene realized that her ten-day trip was about to end. "The place will miss you, too," he told her in a friendly host tone.

"I hope to come back here again someday with my family. They would love it here."

"Your family will be more than welcome at Malloy's Bed and Breakfast anytime," Gene promised.

"I'll remember that." Ngozi bit into an apple. "So was the attractive lady I saw you with the other day your girlfriend? Or am I being too nosey?"

Gene laughed. "She's a good friend," he said simply, not sure if sleeping together qualified them for anything more at the moment.

"I just thought you two looked great together," Ngozi said. "But what do I know?"

Gene gleamed. He recalled that Sloane had actually wondered initially if he was involved with Ngozi. The reality was Sloane was much more his type. He could see his friend Walter being attracted to Ngozi, were he not happily married.

"Could be that your perception is not so far off," Gene told her, leaving it at that. Whatever future he had with Sloane would depend as much on her as him.

Later Gene went to the farmers' market in Kihei to stock up on fresh fruit and vegetables for his guests and food items for himself. Since being in Maui, he'd developed a taste for Hawaiian cuisine, though still very much enjoying the type of meals he'd grown up with which Sloane had mastered so well in the kitchen.

When he got back home, Gene put everything away and set out some macadamia nuts, avocados and banana bread. He shot the breeze with his guests for a bit and then separated himself to phone Sloane, longing to hear her voice following the night of passion they had shared.

"Hi," she answered after the first ring.

"Hey," he said.

"Missed me already?"

"Yeah, I admit it." *More than you know.*

"Missed you, too," Sloane told him.

Gene liked hearing that. "We should do something about it."

"What did you have in mind? Or should I guess?"

A wicked smile played on his lips. "I was thinking I'd like to cook dinner for you tonight."

"Hmm...dinner, huh?" she voiced. "Sure we can even get through a meal without other things happening?"

He chuckled, imagining what sexual mischief they could

get into. "Can't guarantee that," he conceded. "But we can try."

"Or—and I probably shouldn't be saying this—we could skip the meal and get directly to dessert."

Gene practically drooled at the prospect. "I like that idea even better. Can't think of a tastier dessert than you."

"Ditto," she cooed.

"What time do you get off?"

Sloane paused. "I should be off by six. Then I'll stop at the condo and freshen up, and I could be over to your place by around seven-thirty."

"That works for me," he said, counting down the minutes.

"Are you sure I won't distract you from your guests?" she teased.

"Definitely a big distraction." Gene had to be honest. Sloane was one who could easily occupy his attention from anyone and anything else. "But I wouldn't have it any other way. They'll just have to deal with it."

"In that case, we can pick up tonight where we left off last night," Sloane said intrepidly.

"I can hardly wait," he said eagerly.

Sloane couldn't believe she had been so forward with Gene as to her intentions and what she expected from him. The man was a great lover, but he wasn't a machine. Or was he? If their first no-holds-barred sexual experience was any indication, they were both insatiable, with staying power. Could it last? It would take the two of them to find out.

At seven-thirty, Sloane pulled her Toyota Corolla, one of the perks that came with the job, into the driveway of the bed-and-breakfast. She could see that there was a small lot to the side for guests to park. In spite of her comfort level with Gene and vice versa, she wondered if it was really such a good idea to mix their pleasure with his business. Gene's guests should be his top priority. And by the looks of the parking area jammed with rental cars, she was sure that he had a full house.

Sloane resigned herself to playing it by ear. If Gene was overwhelmed as host beyond the breakfast hours, she would quietly back away and wait for a better opportunity. Or she might even offer her assistance, if only to experience how it might be to run a bed-and-breakfast.

After making certain her appearance was up to par, Sloane left the car and went up to the house. The door was slightly ajar. She had a mind to knock but decided to go in, as she was certain that everyone was welcome at Malloy's Bed and Breakfast. Especially the owner's new lover.

Gene greeted Sloane the moment she walked through the door. He looked, for lack of a better description, right at home to her in a gray formfitting polo shirt and dark gray pleated khakis. She picked up the spicy cologne he wore, which pleased her.

"Right on time," he said, grinning.

"Does that surprise you?" she asked playfully.

"Not in the slightest."

Sloane met his eyes deliberately. "So where to from here?"

Gene tilted his head. "My private suite."

"Do you need to check on your guests or anything?"

"If they need something, everyone knows how to reach me. Besides, the guests are pretty self-sufficient and on their own for the most part after breakfast."

"Then I'll have you all to myself," Sloane stated presumptuously.

Gene fixed her with a solid gaze. "Wouldn't have it any other way."

* * *

The master suite was even bigger and nicer than Sloane had imagined. There was a three-piece seating set in an Asian minimalist style and a matching cedar chest and dresser beside a full-length cheval mirror. A cherry pedestal table sat near an oak corner curio cabinet. Across the room there was a wide-screen television and stereo system. Roman shades covered windows on cherry walls, and plush plum carpeting blanketed the floor. She noted the centerpiece of the room was an Edwardian queen sleigh bed.

"Very nice," Sloane said, facing Gene and meeting his eyes.

"I like to be comfortable in my own space," he said, moving up to her. He put his arms around her small waist. "I want you to feel comfortable in here, too."

Sloane shivered at the nearness of him. "I do." *Especially in your presence.*

Gene tilted his face and brushed her lips with his. "Good. Your mouth is so soft and sweet-tasting."

She kissed him lightly. "You think?"

"Very much so." He gave her a longer, mouth-watering kiss and Sloane's knees buckled. "Would you like some wine? I have red, white and raspberry."

Sloane moistened her lips, raising her eyes at him cravingly. "Maybe later. Right now, all I want is your body."

The dimples on Gene's cheeks deepened. "It's all yours for the taking."

"Then I'm taking it now!" She cupped his cheeks and ran her tongue across Gene's mouth before kissing him generously, feeling her desire for this man building to a fevered pitch.

Sloane was shameless with Gene, wanting only to

pleasure him and be pleasured. She locked eyes with him while unzipping his pants. She could see the bulge inside his dark green briefs. Kneeling down, she pulled out his penis so it was directly in front of her face and admired its length and hardness. Deep fudge in color and uncircumcised, it turned Sloane on like never before.

She played with the shaft briefly, slowly running her hands up and down as she felt Gene tense. Good. She wanted him turned on so he was good and ready for her when the time was right. Sloane put the erection in her mouth and moved back and forth, bringing him to the base of her throat. She tickled the tip with her tongue, watching Gene with his eyes squeezed shut and his breath quickened.

She brought her mouth up and down the length of his penis, enjoying the slow seduction, and felt Gene's hands rolling through her hair. Sloane didn't let up as Gene began to quiver and his erection throbbed. His moaning sang to her when she brought him to orgasm, raising her own libido at the same time.

Sloane was lifted to her feet. She peered into Gene's hungry eyes.

"That was wonderful," he said with satisfaction.

"I wanted it to be," she told him, craving more of the man.

"Now it's my turn."

Her eyes locked with his. "Do you want me to keep my clothes on again?"

"Not this time," Gene said salaciously. "I want you naked."

"All right," Sloane replied, wanting the same from him.

"Let me do it," he said.

Gene pulled the V-neck sleeveless black dress over her

shoulders and allowed it to sink to the floor. Sloane was stark naked, aside from the black sandals on her feet. She watched Gene's eyes drink in the sight of her, exploring the contours of her full, rounded breasts, slender waist and curving hips down to her lean legs, and up again.

Instead of feeling self-conscious, Sloane was turned on, wanting him to feast on the sight of her. "Do you like?"

Gene jutted his chin. "You know damned well I do," he spoke huskily.

He lifted her, carried her to the bed, and placed her on the sheets. Removing her shoes, he began massaging her feet with strong and thorough hands. This felt heavenly to Sloane, and it would have been fine if he had kept doing it for some time. Instead, Gene turned his attention elsewhere. He spread her legs and put his face inside. He began licking her, causing Sloane to grip the bed to keep from levitating.

Gene continued his assault on her clitoris with a combination of kisses, sucking, and nibbling. Sloane tried to hold her breath, but only found herself sighing unevenly as she was brought to the brink of coming, only to have Gene hold back as if to deliberately prolong her agony.

Finally, when she could no longer stand it, Sloane grabbed his head and pressed him between her legs, making him finish what he'd started. Gene did not disappoint, caressing her with his tongue and lips masterfully till she exploded in a most fulfilling orgasm. He held her trembling body tightly while she went through the gyrations of reaching her sexual peak and fought to catch her breath.

"I want us to come together now," Sloane pleaded, as her body ached with the strong desire to have him inside her.

"I'm going to make love to you slowly but surely, as it's

meant to be," Gene said in thick voice, quickly removing his clothes and putting on a condom.

Sloane bent her spread knees and put her feet flat on the bed, absorbing Gene's penis as he drove it into her. She thrilled at the tight feel of him and met his powerful thrusts halfway, encouraging him to go deeper and deeper. When he put his chin into her shoulder, she wrapped her hands across his head, her legs around his waist, and put her all into the ride as they made frenetic love.

Their bodies were slick with perspiration and the room temperature was blazing hot in spite of the overhead ceiling fan at work. The scent of sex was in the air, arousing Sloane. She sought out Gene's mouth, kissing him passionately, as she was now on top and riding him like a prized black stallion in a race she refused to lose. Gene seemed of the same mind as he gripped her buttocks, guiding her up and down his erection, propelling himself deep inside her.

Sloane removed her mouth from his and put her breasts in Gene's face, allowing him to suck her nipples as her orgasm drew near. She suppressed a scream, biting down on her lip when it happened. Her contractions around Gene's penis multiplied as Sloane lowered as far as she could onto him, feeling his erection pulsating madly inside her.

They rocked the bed back and forth and smashed their mouths together ardently while achieving victory simultaneously and with total exhilaration. Sloane slumped atop Gene afterward from sheer exhaustion, panting.

"Welcome to Malloy's Bed and Breakfast," Gene said with a breathy chuckle.

Sloane colored, remembering they were not alone there. "I hope your guests weren't disturbed by what was going on in here."

"I doubt they were. Some are still out on the town, others

are too busy doing their own thing to pay much attention to the host's private life."

"Good thing," she joked. "Otherwise, they might think we were certified sex maniacs."

Gene laughed heartily. "Maybe we are." He kissed the side of her head. "You won't hear me complaining. How about you?"

Sloane brought her lips to his. "Not one bit."

"In that case, I say let's just enjoy every inch of each other and to hell what anyone else thinks."

She grinned, finding his philosophy hard to argue with, considering the benefits of their sexual liaison. "It's a deal."

"Shall we seal it?" Gene asked, sliding a hand between her legs.

"Um..." Sloane closed her eyes to the hot sensations and then opened them to see his lascivious gaze upon her. "Why not?"

Never before had Sloane felt so sexually compatible with a man, and it scared her. Were two human beings supposed to click like this in bed? Or had they just gotten extremely lucky to find each other at the right time?

She wondered if there was even more going on here than a blistering sexual connection.

Chapter 6

The next morning, Sloane went for her usual run on the beach. Only this time she was running in the opposite direction, coming from her condo. She had left Gene's place late in the night and was operating on only a few hours' sleep. Gene had wanted her to stay till morning and have breakfast with him and his guests, but she'd decided it would be a bit too awkward. Though she was comfortable with Gene and the intimacy they shared, Sloane was not necessarily ready to ingratiate herself with the guests at his B&B. Especially when she was unsure if their involvement meant something or was purely sexual.

Do I want a relationship with him? Or should we simply continue as is without any pressures?

Sloane bit back the thought. The last thing she wanted was to rock the boat. She increased her running speed, feeling the warm breeze on her face. She loved her job and that had to be her first priority. Period. Forgetting that and allowing herself to become emotionally entangled with someone would only defeat her purpose in coming to Maui to further her career aspirations. Besides, Gene was clearly locked into his bed-and-breakfast right now and not looking for any distraction other than in his bed or hers. She would have to accept it and be thankful that he had come into her life and given her such delightful and unanticipated male friendship with a decided sexual twist. It helped balance Sloane's job, which she was grateful to have and knew that she did well.

After the run, Sloane showered and got dressed for work. She had a quick breakfast of fruit, toast and green tea before heading out. At work, she was briefed on the latest arrivals and what their needs were, taking seriously the hotel's desire to make each and every guest's stay as worry-free and fulfilling as possible.

"Let's see if we can coordinate with the publisher to facilitate some book signings at local bookstores for Bobby Levin," Sloane told Mia, her assistant, while they walked down a long hallway.

Bobby was a former FBI special agent turned mystery novelist who was coming in next month from Colorado to give a seminar at the hotel and promote his latest book about an FBI agent who pursued a serial killer to Maui. Though he planned to sign copies of his book at the seminar, Sloane suspected that more of the locals would be inclined to purchase copies if the author came to them rather than the other way around.

"I'll call the bookstore managers and see what they say," Mia agreed.

"If we're successful, it could result in a favorable recommendation from Mr. Levin of Island Shores as the place to stay for his legions of fans," Sloane said.

Mia rubbed her nose. "I plan to get an autographed copy

of his book. I can always sell it on eBay once my bookshelf is too full."

Sloane smiled. "Good idea." They approached the lobby. "One of our guests has requested that we deliver a case of decaf Kona coffee to his room, saving him the trouble of getting it as a favor to his mother."

"That won't be a problem," Mia said.

Sloane set her sights on the upcoming twenty-five-year class reunion, knowing the event was drawing near. She wanted everyone to have the time of their lives and relive their high school days in style. She imagined it would be fun to have her twenty-year high school reunion in six years in Maui. Might be even better if she had Gene as her handsome escort, assuming their friendship managed to survive the test of time and their respective lives.

The first week of August, Gene welcomed Jean Hourdes from Connecticut to his bed-and-breakfast. Fortysomething with graying, short brunette hair, she was nearly as tall as Gene as they shook hands.

"Aloha and welcome to Malloy's Bed and Breakfast," he told her.

"Thanks. I'm delighted to be here."

"Did you have a good flight?"

"Not bad," she said. "Slept through most it."

"Why don't I show you your room," Gene said, grabbing her bags. "Then I'll introduce you to some of the other guests."

"Sounds wonderful."

He gave her the Ocean Suite, which was the only vacant room at the moment, disregarding the fact that she had paid for a less expensive room.

"What a lovely view," Jean remarked, looking through

the picture window at the Pacific Ocean. A few waves crashed on the beach.

"I feel the same way every time I look out there," Gene agreed. He thought about when the sneaker wave had caught Sloane off guard, allowing him the chance to get to know her in ways that had brightened his entire world.

Jean smiled at him. "It must be so nice to be able to wake up every morning in paradise."

"Yeah, definitely. In fact, I have to pinch myself often to be sure I'm not just dreaming."

She chuckled. "I'm sure you do."

Gene grinned. He was used to the awe guests showed when first arriving in Maui. Everyone seemed to think that with all the beauty and serenity of the islands, life there was problem-free. The truth was, even Maui fell short of utopia. It was what you did with the opportunities afforded there that made all the difference in the world.

"So what are your plans during your stay in Maui?" he asked her routinely.

"Lie on the beach and get a really nice tan so when I go back to Connecticut all of my friends will drool with envy."

"Well, you've come to the right place at the right time," Gene remarked. "Just be sure to use plenty of sunscreen so you don't get a bad sunburn."

"I sure will," she said.

Two hours later, Gene drove into Lahaina, where his friend, Neil Nagamine, operated a dinner cruise. The cruise seemed like something Sloane might enjoy. Gene had only been on it once, but never forgot the experience of going out on the ocean and witnessing breathtaking sunset views and the night lights of Maui and its neighboring islands, Molokai and Lanai.

Gene stepped inside the small office that housed the

Maui Seas Supper Cruise. He immediately spotted Neil, an Okinawan who was hard to miss with his hefty frame and long jet-black hair pulled into a ponytail. The two became fast friends when Gene first moved to Maui, often sending business to one another. Networking was something Gene considered extremely important in making contacts and letting potential guests know about his bed-and-breakfast, available now or to keep in mind for their next visit.

Neil broke into a big grin when he saw Gene. "Well, look what the tide brought in."

"And I still managed to stay on my feet," Gene said with a laugh. He gave the taller man a handshake and a hug. "How are you these days?"

"No complaints. At least none that knock me off my feet. What about you?"

Gene blinked. "I'm good."

"So the bed-and-breakfast is reeling them in?" asked Neil.

"We're getting our fair share of guests—some of them thanks to your recommendations."

"And vice versa," Neil said.

Gene smiled. "Everyone loves the idea of a dinner cruise on the ocean."

"Not everyone. Some people don't realize they get seasick till they do. Then it all comes back to me."

"I'm sure you know just how to smooth the waters, so to speak," Gene told him. "That's what we do to try and keep our guests happy."

Neil jutted his chin. "Yeah, I guess so."

"I'm thinking about taking the cruise myself." Gene moved up to the counter. "Actually, I'd like to bring a lady I've been spending time with."

Neil's eyes lit. "Really? Must be serious."

Gene cracked a grin. "Not in so many words," he said,

careful to keep his relationship with Sloane in a proper perspective in spite of how comfortable he felt when he was with her. "We're just hanging out and having a good time. I believe she'd really enjoy the cruise."

Neil eyed him thoughtfully. "So she's a local?"

"She is now. Sloane just moved here from North Carolina. She works at the Island Shores."

"Your five-star resort competition?" Neil's gaze expanded. "You sure she isn't more than you can handle?"

Gene's head rolled back as he laughed heartily. "I think I can hold my own. She's pretty down-to-earth, competition aside."

"In that case, I say go for it with the cruise and let her see how we treat people we care for in Maui."

Gene nodded enthusiastically. "Let's do it," he said presumptively. "I'd like to make reservations and give Sloane an experience that she won't soon forget."

He doubted it would leave his memory anytime soon either. Everything Gene did with Sloane left a lasting impression on him, especially when they made love. He hoped this was just the beginning of the wonderful experiences they were creating together with no end in sight.

The next day, Gene went to the Island Shores hotel, hoping to steal a few minutes of Sloane's time and tell her about the dinner cruise, assuming it was something she'd want to do with him. Even then, he was already contemplating other adventures they might try in the future, regardless of how either chose to define their relationship or what they hoped to get out of in the future.

At 6:30 p.m., Sloane was in Reception Room A for the Beaubien High School twenty-five-year class reunion. She was there not only as a representative of the hotel but as an invited guest. The organizer of the event, Sylvia Bonner, had stayed at the last hotel where Sloane worked and they had become acquainted then.

"Looks like everyone showed up and then some," Sylvia told Sloane as guests mingled and a local band played nostalgic music.

Sloane smiled at the petite blonde in her early forties. "Not too surprising. How often does one get to reunite with old friends in Hawaii?"

"True. Except that some old friends would rather relive memories in their heads and not in person."

"I suppose some memories are best left alone," Sloane agreed. She had mostly positive memories from high school and had kept herself in great shape since then. That obviously wasn't the case for everyone and was a perfect excuse to avoid such occasions like the plague.

Sloane found herself wondering what Gene's high school years had been like. Given his physical specimen of a body, she imagined he'd been a jock while maintaining an active lifestyle.

"Oh, there's my high school beau, Victor Hamilton," gushed Sylvia. Sloane eyed a gray-haired man of medium build wearing a Beaubien High jersey. "I can't believe how little he's changed."

Sloane smiled. "Better go catch up on old times...and maybe make some new memories," she told her, knowing that Sylvia was recently divorced and on the prowl.

Sylvia sighed heavily. "At this point, I'm open for anything—so long as he's not married and hoping to get lucky."

Sloane watched her amble across the room toward the one who apparently got away. Or was it the other way around?

She certainly wasn't interested in being with a married

man. She preferred a man like Gene, who was happily single as a successful professional and very interested in spending his spare time with her. Much of that time lately had been spent in bed, where they continued to find new ways to make love. Sloane didn't want to look beyond what they had going for them at the moment for fear of jinxing a good thing. She assumed Gene felt the same way in not pushing things.

"Are you daydreaming about the good old days?" Sloane heard the deep whisper in her ear.

She looked over her shoulder and saw Gene's handsome face, catching her by surprise. "What are you doing here?"

"Thought I'd crash the party after learning that you might be here," he responded evenly. "Looks like I hit pay dirt."

Sloane warmed as she caught the glint of his penetrating eyes on her. "That you did," she said. "I was just checking in to make sure everything was going according to plan."

"And is it?"

"Yes, so far so good."

"Except that you look like a fish out of water trying to fit in," Gene said with amusement.

Self-consciousness swept over her face. "Is it that obvious?"

"Probably only to someone who feels exactly the same way," Gene said with a chuckle. "Crashing parties is not usually my thing. But I felt it was worth it to see if I could track down the hotel's director of guest relations."

Sloane's cheeks rose. "So you're here for official business?"

"Actually, very personal," he responded sensually.

She reacted to the words and man. "Now is not the time..."

He angled his head. "Don't worry. I'm not here to jump your bones or take you away from your duties." Gene grinned seductively. "I was wondering if you had dinner plans for tomorrow night."

"Just some leftover spaghetti and meatballs," Sloane said. "Why?"

"Oh, I was hoping you might like to have dinner with me on a supper cruise."

"Sounds interesting." *Not to mention incredibly romantic.* "Tell me more..."

"A friend of mine runs the cruise, and the views are out of this world," Gene told her. "The actual dinner is pretty damned good, too."

Sloane met his eyes curiously. "So you've been on the cruise before?"

He gave her a straight look. "It'll feel like the first time with you."

"Good response," she said with a smile. He certainly knew how to make her seem special to him. It also sounded like another way to explore Maui and the man. "Okay, I'm in."

A half grin played on Gene's lips. "Cool."

"Are you always so full of surprises?" Sloane asked.

"Not always. Let's just say that I like spending time with you and taking advantage of some of the wonders and treats of the island at the same time."

Sloane smiled. "It works for me." How could it not, when he was so sexy and romantic in his overtures?

Gene raised a brow as the band began playing a slow number. "I love that song," he said, taking her hands. "Looks like there's an open spot for us on the dance floor. Can I get a dance before I leave you alone?"

Sloane glanced at the area where a few couples were slow dancing. She cast her eyes at Gene and felt a tingling sensation from his large hands covering hers. Though she was still on duty and Gene wasn't on the guest list, one quick dance with the best-looking, sexiest man in the room wouldn't hurt.

"One dance should be fine," she told him.

"Then let's get out there and show them how it's done."

Sloane had her arms around Gene's neck while he held her waist as they moved in slow, sensual circles. She liked the way he smelled, always a manly mixture of his scent and expensive cologne. Moreover, she felt comfortable in his sturdy arms. They were as in sync on the dance floor as in bed. With her eyes closed and their bodies aligned, Sloane almost felt like they were all by themselves, dancing to their own heartbeats.

"You're good," Gene said, seemingly echoing her sentiments.

"You're not so bad yourself," she uttered.

"That's because I'm dancing with by far the most attractive woman at the class reunion."

Sloane blushed. "Such sweet words."

"And an even sweeter dance partner," he murmured.

Her eyes rose to meet his. Sloane really wanted to kiss him, tossing away any qualms about the setting where neither of them belonged. She opened her lips and brought them to Gene's waiting mouth.

He followed her lead, pulling their bodies closer and giving Sloane the type of kiss she sought from him. She loved the hard persuasion of his lips and was sure he got as much satisfaction from the kiss she laid on him. Sloane grew light-headed as the kiss made her feel like she was walking on air. She'd become lost in the moment when Gene pulled back. Only then had Sloane realized the band had stopped playing.

"That was very enjoyable," Gene said, and licked his lips.

"Seems like we can't get enough of that these days," she admitted, tasting him on her mouth as well, still feeling the sensations of the kiss.

Gene smiled. "Guess some things are just meant to be."

"You think so, do you?" She batted her eyes at him, even if she was starting to agree where they were concerned.

"Yeah. But right now, I'm taking you away from your duties." He held her cheeks and kissed the top of Sloane's head. "I'll let you get back to it and talk to you tomorrow."

Sloane was reluctant to let him go. But she also knew he was the type of distraction that could cause her to lose track of time and space. This was still her workplace, and she wasn't off the clock.

"Thanks for dropping by and inviting me on the supper cruise," she told him, her voice high.

"Anytime," Gene said earnestly.

Sloane watched him walk away, his tight buns enviable. She liked them even better when they weren't covered by trousers and briefs, conjuring up naughty thoughts brought on by the man himself and their passionate kiss.

"That was some kiss," Sylvia said, approaching Sloane.

Sloane was embarrassed. "I hope everyone wasn't watching."

"They would have to be blind to miss it," Sylvia said with a grin.

"I didn't mean to upstage your class reunion—"

"You didn't." Sylvia laughed. "I'm just teasing. It's perfectly all right if you had a little romance with your man. That's what this reunion is all about, if one is fortunate enough to have that kind of chemistry with someone from yesteryear or the present."

"Thanks for saying that," Sloane said, knowing the chemistry between her and Gene was abundant and dripping with sexuality. "But what about your reunion with your high school beau?"

Sylvia frowned. "Not happening. It was great to see Victor again, but he's about to get married to his longtime girlfriend, who happens to be here too."

"Sorry to hear that."

"Don't be. We had our moment back in the day. It wasn't meant to be this time around." Sylvia tasted the drink in her hand. "On a more positive note, I am talking with another former classmate who I had the biggest crush on in high school. He's single and we seem to be clicking, so we'll see what happens."

Sloane offered her a nice smile. "Wonderful. Hope it works out."

"Same to you and that devilishly handsome man who commanded your attention," said Sylvia. "Though, from the looks of that lip lock, I'd say you're well on your way."

Sloane let that sink in, while wondering where this very hot romance with Gene was leading. Was she ready to move into a full-fledged relationship? Was he? Or should she not think too much about the future and simply enjoy the moment and the man?

Chapter 7

Sloane and Gene climbed aboard the 118-foot luxury touring yacht for the Maui Seas supper cruise. Sloane was excited, as she had always wanted to go on a cruise, though this was a much shorter one than she had envisioned. But it was a start. The fact that her date was Gene made it even more romantic being out on the water. He seemed very comfortable introducing her to different aspects of Maui, and she welcomed the attention from someone who had become a part of the community and seemed to relish it.

They walked along with other guests onto the roomy observation deck as the captain spoke about the ship.

"Power comes from four GM 12V71TI engines, allowing for a cruising speed of twenty knots," he explained, tugging at his gray beard. "A Naiad gyroscopically controlled stabilizing system allows for a smooth, relaxing ride. We have room for one hundred and forty-nine passengers. The yacht is perfectly suited for sightseeing and inter-island cruising on the Pacific. You'll find a snack bar and a first-rate cocktail lounge for your pleasure as we head out."

A few minutes later the yacht pulled out of Lahaina Harbor, slip number three.

"Well, this should be fun," Gene said, gazing down at Sloane. His cheeks dimpled as he smiled. "And romantic, too."

She relished the thought, smiling back. "I'm looking forward to it."

"So am I."

Sloane nearly melted from the intensity of his gaze. She sighed, determined to enjoy the experience without reading too much into the way Gene took her breath away, even though she didn't think it was intentional on his part. Or was every facial gesture, lilt of his voice and move he made totally calculating?

They sat at a table on the open-air upper dining deck. They had been served Hawaiian pineapple-glazed prime rib, fresh green salad, mixed vegetables and dinner rolls, along with white wine.

"See what you've been missing all this time?" Gene said while slicing into the prime rib.

"You mean you in my life?" Sloane asked, half joking.

"That, too!" He flashed a serious look. "But I meant the many wonders of Maui."

You're one of those wonders. She smiled at him over her wineglass. "I've missed a lot," she conceded. Sloane put down her glass and gazed out at the water. Her eyes moved up to the sky where numerous stars twinkled overhead, as if they were winking at her. "It's gorgeous."

"So are you," Gene said. "But I think I've probably told you that enough already."

She chuckled. "A girl can never be told too many times

that she's gorgeous," Sloane said. "Thank you for the compliment."

"It's no effort at all on my part, since I'm only saying what my eyes can plainly see."

Not wanting to get too full of herself, Sloane changed the subject. "So when you're not playing host at a bed-and-breakfast or showing a lady a good time, what do you do?"

"Lots of things," Gene answered vaguely.

"Such as?"

"I like to swim, play tennis, drive, watch sports, listen to music…"

Sloane spooned some vegetables, her interest piqued. She realized that though she had come to know Gene intimately and as a businessman, she really knew painfully little about his makeup. And vice versa. "What type of music do you like?" she asked, figuring him for a Motown sound or maybe a blues man.

"Mostly standards and classical music," he replied. "But I also enjoy some contemporary jazz, easy listening, soul and a little blues."

Well, at least I was partially correct. "Interesting mix."

"I like to mix it up." Gene cracked a cute smile.

"What about Hawaiian music?"

"Actually, I do like Hawaiian music, especially island jazz, hula and traditional South Pacific."

Sloane's eyes grew with admiration. "Wow, you know your stuff."

Gene laughed. "You get to the longer you live here."

"I suppose." She nibbled on a roll.

"What do you like to do outside of work, besides running?" Gene was curious.

"I enjoy photography, read literature and women's fiction, watch public broadcasting and, guiltily, some reality TV. I also like to play on the computer."

He gave a thoughtful nod. "Sounds like you have a number of ways to keep yourself occupied."

"I guess everyone does these days," she said, sipping some water.

"What type of photographs do you take?"

"Mostly landscapes and people. I hope to add some seascapes to my collection soon."

Gene smiled. "I'd love to see some of your photographs."

"Really?" Sloane was surprised he would be interested in that side of her.

"Yes, I'm into pictures, especially scenic ones. And since you're the photographer, it should make them even more appealing."

She soaked in the flattery. "Most of what I've taken is still back in Raleigh," she told him regrettably. "But I have a few photographs that I can show you."

"Wonderful."

Sloane looked out at the water and the colorful lights of the other islands. "So is that view."

Gene grinned. "Yeah, I thought you would find it mesmerizing."

"I do," she said, thinking that he was every bit as enchanting to her. Not to mention probably the sexiest man alive. Certainly in Hawaii. Getting to know Gene better made him all the more appealing. She faced him. "Have you lived anywhere other than Detroit or Maui?"

He tasted the drink. "As a matter of fact, I have. I spent a few years at Michigan State University in East Lansing, where I got my degree. And I also lived in Houston for a year and Cleveland for three months."

"So you got around," hummed Sloane.

"A little."

"Why three months in Cleveland?" she asked curiously.

Gene sat back. "I was sent there for an assignment in my former life in marketing."

Sloane cocked a brow. "That's a big jump from marketing to bed-and-breakfast proprietor."

"Not really. In both, you have to sell a product and be available to see it through, while hoping to make a profit."

"Good point," she said.

"Yeah, I think so." He set his eyes upon her. "And where else have you set up shop besides Raleigh?"

"Well, let's see…I got my degree from the University of North Carolina at Chapel Hill, spent a year in Nairobi, Kenya, as an exchange student, and I lived in New York for a while."

"Kenya, huh? Interesting."

"I thought it was," she said.

"Now you're living the laid-back life in Maui," Gene said with a grin.

"Looks that way." Sloane smiled.

"My good fortune."

She held his gaze. "Who says it's only yours?"

Gene's eyes glimmered and he lifted his wineglass for a toast.

Sloane followed suit, feeling as though she'd made a real connection on the island and was in no hurry to see it fall by the wayside anytime soon.

After they finished dinner, they made their way to what was billed as the "largest floating dance floor." Picking up right where they'd left off at the class reunion, Sloane fell into Gene's arms and their bodies swayed to the sultry

Hawaiian music. She was aware of every inch of him, certain the same was true in reverse.

"Where did you learn to dance like this?" Gene whispered in her ear.

Sloane felt his tepid breath on her cheek. "I could ask you the same thing."

"So ask."

"All right," she took the bait. "Just how many women have you used your charms on while dancing in this romantic setting?" She could imagine that virtually any woman could be swept off her feet by Gene, particularly while caught up in the romantic atmosphere of Maui.

Gene pulled her a little closer. "None that can hold a candle to you."

"Cute answer, but it didn't really answer my question."

"Do I detect a little jealousy?"

Sloane snickered. "In your dreams."

"The only one in my dreams these days is you," he said.

"Hmm," she voiced with misgiving. "I'm not so sure about that."

"Maybe this will help convince you…"

Gene suddenly tilted her in midsong and laid a solid kiss on Sloane's mouth that left her knees buckling. She was sure that had Gene not held her firmly, she might well have taken a fall.

Sloane sucked on his lower lip, his upper lip, and back again, caught up in the soulful kiss and the man dispensing it. Gene's tongue whipped in and out of her mouth, leaving behind the taste of his dinner wine. Just when Sloane began to feel her head spinning and body tingling with excitement, Gene pulled her back up.

"Now what were we saying about other women?" he asked her with amusement.

Sloane caught her breath. "Forget I asked the question."

"Consider it forgotten. And, just for the record, I don't make a habit of taking women on romantic cruises any more than you make a habit of accepting such invitations."

"I get it," she said, feeling a little foolish that she'd asked him about other women. Especially when they weren't committed to one another enough to start dictating whom one could and could not see. Then why was she beginning to feel like she wanted things to be exclusive between them? Maybe because she had a feeling he shared those same sentiments.

"When the ship docks, let's continue this at your place," Gene said, peering down at her.

Sloane met his eyes and felt as though she were reading his mind. He wanted her in bed. Or the next closest thing. They were definitely on the same page.

"I'm game if you are." The words came out of her mouth longingly.

He grinned seductively. "Oh, yes, very game."

When they arrived at Sloane's condo, they couldn't get their clothes off fast enough, each ripping away at the other's till both were naked. In bed, Sloane and Gene kissed passionately, peppering each other's mouths, cheeks, chins, ears and necks with hot and lustful kisses and nibbles as they warmed up for what was to come.

Gene was eager to put his face between Sloane's legs, wanting to take in her intoxicating scent, feel her crown jewel between his lips and drive her wild with desire for him. He pried his mouth from hers and trailed hot kisses down her body until he reached her most sensitive area.

She wrapped her thighs around his neck and implored him through her soft murmurs to give her an orgasm. He was happy to comply, and it turned him on madly when she was aroused.

Gene flicked his tongue across her clitoris and Sloane cried out each time he touched her, making him want to do so time and time again. She got very wet for him, letting herself go without holding back.

"You taste better each time," he uttered lasciviously.

"It's because you make me come when you do that…so masterfully," Sloane murmured.

Gene continued to stimulate her with his mouth, gratified with her feverish reaction, even as his erection ached to be inside of her. He knew she was tight and more than ready for him.

Though she kept his head wedged between her legs, Sloane managed to contort her body so that she was able to take Gene's penis into her mouth. He exhaled a deep breath as her tongue rolled across the tip, making him barely able to contain himself. He enjoyed the exquisite agony while continuing to orally satisfy Sloane. Their pleasure was intense, leaving both shuddering as their orgasms came simultaneously.

Gene extricated himself from between Sloane's thighs. He wanted to be deep inside her body. He watched her mouth come up off his penis and saw the raw need for him in her lustful eyes.

"Please make love to me and don't hold back!" Her voice was demanding.

Watching Sloane lying there with her legs spread tantalizingly and a fingertip placed sexily in her mouth drove Gene mad with craving. "I couldn't hold back even if I wanted to," he told her zealously.

He stretched his arm down to his pants on the floor and pulled out the foil packet, tearing it open and removing the condom. After sliding it onto his erection, Gene mounted Sloane's waiting body and propelled himself inside her. He drove into her hard and hungry as her legs wrapped high around his back.

"Go deeper," Sloane shouted, arching her body and bringing it up to slam into his with each powerful thrust. "Don't stop!"

"Let's both not stop," Gene said heavily. "Not till we get there..."

His eyes shut when Sloane's measured contractions brought Gene a new level of pleasure while his erection went as deep as it could go. He licked her tautened nipples back and forth as she cried out and then grabbed his cheeks and covered his mouth with her breathy kiss.

They had sex for another half hour, changing positions and untangling arms and legs while seizing each and every moment of passion as though there were no more tomorrow. Their bodies dripped with moisture and the sounds of lovemaking filled the room.

Sloane was on top as her climax arrived. She fell onto Gene, quivering wildly and seeking out his mouth in a torrent of kisses. He held her waist firmly, guiding Sloane deeper onto his penis while his surge came thunderously. Gene buried his face in the valley of Sloane's slick breasts, feeling her heart pounding as the climax worked its way through every part of his body.

When they were done, Gene sucked in a deep breath, wanting only to hold Sloane and come back down to earth. He was sure that sex had never been this good before. And he couldn't imagine it ever being this good with anyone again.

Could Sloane say the same?

* * *

Sloane breathed in the sexual scent in the air as she lay beside Gene, their arms and legs wrapped around each other after another night of passion and pleasure. She couldn't get enough of him and clearly he felt the same way about her based on his actions. But as much as she wanted to think this was all about sex, sex and more sex, Sloane knew there was more going on than that. Certainly on her part. She hadn't been looking for anything serious. Not at this time in her life with the challenges of her new job.

Gene Malloy was causing her to seriously rethink her position. She wasn't in this alone, though. She had to know where his mind was. Sloane already knew where his body was, having gotten to know every intimate detail of it. She just wasn't sure that was enough any longer, even as the thought of making love to Gene set her soul and body on fire.

Sloane tilted her head to look at Gene's striking face. He too seemed quietly contemplative now that the sighs and moans they had emitted earlier had subsided. "So where are we going with this?" she asked.

Gene lowered his eyes to connect with hers. "You mean our relationship?"

"Is that what it is?" Her lashes fluttered. Neither had really defined what it was they were engaged in.

"What do you want it to be?"

She glared at him. "Come on now, that's not fair. I'm asking you the question. Please don't turn it around on me."

His jaw tightened. "All right. We're obviously involved in more than a one-night stand. I suppose we are seeing each other or dating." He met her gaze. "Is that what you wanted to hear?"

Sloane pursed her lips, happy to know he saw things as she did to an extent, but feeling unsatisfied for some reason. "I only want to know how you really feel about us," she responded. "Not what you think I want to hear."

He chuckled. "Well, I'm not sure what you want me to say."

She drew in a deep breath. "Do you see a future between us?"

"I thought you were only looking for fun and sexual frolic, nothing serious?"

"Maybe I was—then."

His gaze remained focused on her face. "And now…?"

Sloane considered this carefully. She didn't want to give him the wrong signal. Or seem wishy-washy. At the same time, it was a woman's prerogative to change her position midstream. And a man's, too.

"I think I want to build something steady between us and see where it goes from there." *Okay, I've put it out there. Now the rest is up to you.*

"I'd like that, too," Gene said equably.

"Seriously…?"

"Yeah, but…"

"Always a but," she cut in with irritation. "But what?"

He lifted his leg off hers. "I can't promise you anything like an official commitment."

"That's not what I'm asking for," she said tartly.

"You're sure about that?" Doubt rang in his voice.

"Yes. I just wanted to know that our heads were in the same place in wanting to be together."

"I definitely want to be with you," Gene said honestly. "You're everything I could ask for in a woman. But, putting my cards on the table, I've already been through a marriage and I'm not really looking to go down that road again. I just want things to continue as they are."

"Who said anything about marriage?" Sloane rolled her eyes. "No one's asking you to sign away your bachelorhood in blood. I didn't come to Maui to get married, if that's what you're worried about."

"I'm not worried," he insisted. "I only wanted to put it out there so we understand each other."

"I think I'm beginning to understand all too well." She untangled herself from his body, suddenly feeling unsettled about the limitations of this arrangement. "You want all the goodies of a hot and passionate sexual relationship, but only on your terms."

"Seems to me that we entered into this with the same terms. Or am I mistaken?"

"Maybe we did," she conceded. "It doesn't mean I'm forever locked into that position. I was hoping you felt the same. If not, then I'm sorry."

"I'm sorry, too, if I've offended you," he said sincerely. "That was never my intention. To be clear, I'm not locked into anything, except for wanting to be with you. I simply think that there's no reason to rock the cart by looking too far ahead. Let's just take it a day at a time."

Sloane suddenly realized that she might have been expecting too much, too soon from him. They hadn't been involved for that long and they both needed time to see if this was truly headed in the right direction or if it would burn itself out before either could end up hurt and disillusioned.

"Sure, why not?" Sloane told him, knowing she had her job to fall back on in case things with Gene stalled. "I wouldn't want any apples to fall out of that cart."

Gene grinned seductively. "You're the apple of my eye."

She felt his awareness of her. "You would say that while we're naked in bed."

"That can't be helped, now can it?"

Sloane blinked. "If you say so."

"I think we both say so."

Gene ran his hand across her breast and nipple. Sloane couldn't ignore how good it felt. When he put his hand between her legs, her ire with him began to melt like hot butter. No matter her misgivings, she couldn't resist Gene when he put her in the mood. Perhaps he was playing on that in keeping what they had alive and well while shying away from something more substantive. And she was totally falling for it, just as she was falling for the man himself.

Gene spent the night at Sloane's place, though they did little sleeping. She was the one woman with whom he could make love for hours on end and still be left wanting more. What he didn't know was if this meant what they had constituted the basis for a long-term relationship. Sloane had caught him off guard in wondering where things were headed. He probably hadn't handled it as well as he should have.

The truth was, he liked being with her. Apart from the sex, she was good company, something that had been sorely lacking in his life for a while now. But he wasn't quite sure what it meant. Could what they had developed in bed lead to a much deeper commitment down the line?

Was marriage a possibility in the future, in spite of what he had suggested to Sloane? Or was that a road she had no interest in herself as an independent businesswoman who obviously had chosen not to settle down with anyone?

Gene didn't care to speculate at the moment, hoping that they had sufficiently smoothed the waters while making the most of their time together. He was holding Sloane's naked body, her alluring scent and taste lingering on his lips. Though they had practically worn each other out making love, he suspected they might still have one more round in them before it was time to go back to the bed-and-breakfast and cater to his guests and their needs.

Chapter 8

Sloane made her rounds the following day, welcoming new guests and greeting current ones. In both instances, she wanted to show them the hospitality of Island Shores. It was why she'd been brought there, to uphold a tradition established ever since the resort hotel opened for business. Still fresh on Sloane's mind was her conversation with Gene last night, before, during and after their lovemaking. It was still a mystery to her as to how far he wanted their relationship to go in the future. Clearly, he was not interested in marrying again, soured by his past experience. Indeed, Sloane had seen her fair share of marriages turned into divorce, affairs and unhappiness. Yes, she knew there were others who were successful in maintaining a long marriage and managed to keep the fires of bliss burning. But they seemed to be the exception rather than the rule these days.

It doesn't mean I'd have to go down the same path

if I met the man of my dreams who happened to be the marrying type.

Gene came the closest to marriage material Sloane had ever been involved with for a woman for whom marriage had never been a priority. She'd always been too busy to want to think in those terms. And now that the idea of being a wife had entered her mind, the timing and man were off. Maybe something was telling her to keep that genie in the bottle and be happy that she had her career and a great lover. Not to mention living in as picturesque a setting as she could have ever dreamed.

"Aloha," a woman said, getting Sloane's attention.

She saw a thirtysomething couple standing there dressed casually and greeted them.

"Can you recommend a great place to have dinner outside the hotel?" asked the man.

Sloane smiled. "I sure can," she responded, as two such places came to mind. "I think the Kaanapali Beach luau is a terrific choice for a fabulous dinner and great show. Or if you prefer a more romantic setting, you might want to try the Maui Seas supper cruise. The food is excellent and the views are incredible." Aware that some visitors were more budget-conscious, she also recommended a couple of less expensive restaurants.

A few minutes later, Sloane ran into Sally Weincroft, the seventy-five-year-old Australian who had asked the hotel to set up her itinerary.

"G'day," Sally said in a sprightly tone.

"Good day." Sloane flashed her teeth at the woman, who was slender with fine white hair and seemingly the picture of health. It was her third day in Maui. "How are things going?"

"Marvelous. I'm having the time of my life, thanks to you and your staff."

Sloane blushed. "We're just doing our jobs."

"You're doing it well. I will tell my family and friends back in Sydney when I go home that they must visit Maui and stay at the Island Shores Resort."

"Any recommendations are always appreciated," Sloane told her.

Sally took a digital camera out of her purse. "Do you mind if I take a picture of you with me?"

Sloane's mouth curved upward. "Of course you can."

She hugged Sally and posed for the picture as Sally stretched her arm out and snapped the shot.

"Thanks so much," Sally said. "It will add to my memories of this wonderful island."

"Happy to do whatever I can to help," Sloane said, and waved as Sally moved away.

A moment later Sloane was joined by Alan Komoda. "Based on her outfit, I'd say Sally has easily fit right in with us Hawaiians," he said.

"I think you're right," Sloane said, noting Sally's colorful Maui T-shirt and print shorts.

"Hopefully she'll be influential in getting more people from Down Under to come here."

Sloane gave him a knowing look. "I think there's a very good chance of that."

Alan nodded and then frowned. "It looks like some kids trashed a suite before they checked out."

"My goodness," Sloane uttered. "How bad is it?"

"Bad enough. All I can say is they must have had some wild party in there."

"Do you want me to—?"

"I've taken care of it," Alan said. "The damages and extra cleanup are being billed to the party who reserved the room."

Sloane sighed. "That's good."

"Unfortunately, we get a few of those every year. Seems like a tropical paradise mixed with drinking leads to rowdy behavior for some people."

"Those types don't need a tropical setting to act crazy," Sloane said. Still, she wondered if Gene ever had these problems at his bed-and-breakfast. If so, how did he deal with them? Was he able to spot potential troublemakers in advance?

The next day, Sloane had tea with Kendra in one of the Island Shore's three restaurants, The Leaf Garden.

"Edy and I went out again last night," Kendra gushed. "Then I spent the night at his place. That man must have invented the word stamina."

"Didn't waste any time, I see," Sloane teased as she thought about Gene's incredible stamina in bed, which she matched step for step.

"And it's a good thing," Kendra said with a smile. "The band is doing a gig in Kauai next weekend, so it will have to carry us till he gets back."

Sloane smiled. "Sounds like you really have the hots for him. Or is it the other way around?"

"It's both. We like hanging out—just like someone else I know."

Sloane's cheeks flushed. "Wonder who that might be?"

"You tell me." Kendra batted her lashes. "Or have things cooled off between you and Mr. Bed-and-Breakfast hunk?"

"No, things have not cooled off between us." Sloane put the teacup to her lips. "Quite the contrary, it seems to be getting better all the time in the bedroom."

"What about outside the bedroom?" Kendra asked.

"Things are good there, too." Sloane envisioned being in Gene's arms on the dance floor.

"So the sex is great, the friendship is fantastic, the man walks on water—sounds like someone you'll want to hang on to for a long time. Or am I reading you wrong?"

"I didn't say he walked on water," Sloane said, chuckling. "Well, maybe close to it. That doesn't mean we're in this for the long haul."

"Doesn't he feel the same way about you?" Kendra asked.

"I guess…" Sloane sighed. "I'm not sure where we're headed, if anywhere. He's divorced and not interested in marriage. I'm single and open to—"

"Whoa—" Kendra's eyes widened. "You've already got marriage on your mind?"

"I didn't say that."

"But you aren't denying it?"

"All I'm saying is that I'm keeping my options open," Sloane said. "What will be, will be, whether it's a long relationship or…whatever."

"But what if you two aren't on the same page?" Kendra asked curiously.

Sloane paused. How would she handle that? If she decided she wanted more than an out-of-this-world sexual relationship, would Gene come around to her way of thinking? Or was his position set in stone regarding tying the knot again someday? Sloane imagined the whole issue was probably all for naught since she was still holding true to her own plan of succeeding in her career and not allowing something such as marriage to detract from it. Or had her resolve begun to weaken, whether she cared to admit it or not?

"Then I suppose I might need to find a new book,"

she remarked, though doubting it would come to that anytime soon.

Kendra grinned crookedly. "In that case, good thing there are lots of great reads out there in the form of eligible, gorgeous men."

Sloane could barely conceive that anyone could captivate her the way Gene had. She only hoped it wasn't the recipe to set her up for a fall.

Sloane's cell phone rang. She took it out of her purse and saw that it was Gene calling. Should she answer it?

"Don't mind me," Kendra told her. "While you're passing sweet words to your man, I'll text Edy. He loves it when I tell him how hot he is."

"Okay." Sloane clicked on the phone. "Hi."

"Hey," he said. "Busy?"

"Not right now." She took a sip of tea, happy to hear his sexy voice.

"My buddy, Walter, from Detroit and his wife, Talia, are flying in this weekend for their anniversary."

"How nice," Sloane said thoughtfully. "I take it they'll be staying at your B&B?"

"Yeah." Gene paused. "If you don't mind, I was thinking that it would be nice if you spent some time with Talia, maybe show her around a bit."

"I'd be happy to do that."

"Thanks. I'm sure they will be googoo-gagaing each other most of the time, but that might grow old, and I just want them to have a good time."

"Does anyone ever not have a good time when visiting Maui?" questioned Sloane. She wondered if he had always been so cynical about romance between a husband and wife. Or had his perception changed after his divorce?

"Probably not," Gene allowed. "I guess I thought this

would be a great opportunity for my best friend's wife to hang out with my girlfriend."

Sloane's brow rose when she heard him describe her as his girlfriend. "So I'm your girlfriend now?"

He chuckled with embarrassment. "Do you have a problem with that?"

Sloane glanced at Kendra, who seemed to be hanging on every word. "Not if you don't."

"I don't," Gene said. "In fact, I like the sound of it."

So did she. At least it gave them a foundation to build on. "I'll try to think of something special to do with Talia," she told him. "Do you know what kinds of things she enjoys?"

"She's a runner," Gene mentioned. "Talia would probably find it a big thrill to run alongside the ocean. Just be sure to stay away from those sneaker waves," he added with a laugh.

"I'm sure we will." Sloane forced a smile, though she wished someone had given her the same advice beforehand. "Anything else?"

"Talia loves to shop. Walter tells me she's never entered a store she didn't like. No telling how much she'll run up the charge cards while here."

"I know a couple of stores she'd probably like." Sloane thought it might be the perfect time for her to build up her own wardrobe, as she had been too busy to do much shopping for nonessential clothing to this point.

"Sounds good," Gene said. "You and Talia will get along great. You'll definitely leave an impression on her."

"Hope you haven't gotten too carried away in your praise," Sloane told him and saw Kendra suppressing a giggle. "I'm not sure I want to be put on a pedestal." Certainly not by trying to impress his friends.

Gene laughed easily. "Don't worry, I managed to contain

my enthusiasm where you're concerned. Walter and Talia are very down-to-earth people. They're also close friends and always like to know how I'm doing, who I'm seeing, what she's like—all that stuff."

"I see." Sloane thought about her friend Gail, in whom she'd confided about Gene and who always wanted to know more. Not to mention Kendra, who had finished her text and was seemingly itching for Sloane to hang up and fill her in on the details. "I'm looking forward to meeting your friends." Maybe they could even give her a few tidbits about the man that he had chosen not to provide.

"I can assure you the feeling is mutual." His voice dropped a charming octave, causing Sloane to react. "I'll let you get back to what you were doing."

"All right," she agreed, even if she would have loved to talk longer and more about their relationship.

"Talk to you later," he said and made a kissing sound that managed to reach through the phone and warm Sloane's soul.

Gene was a trifle nervous as he watched through the window for the rental car to pull into the driveway. It wasn't every day that someone from his hometown visited. In fact, he could probably count on one hand those who had and stayed at the bed-and-breakfast, and that didn't include Walter and Talia Griffin. Till now.

He wished Sloane were there with him to greet them, but understood that she was busy working. At least she was willing to get together with them and show Talia around. Gene was glad they seemed to have gotten past a small bump in the road and were moving to a new level of dating. He had referred to Sloane for the first time as his girlfriend, a term that he hadn't used since before his marriage. He liked the sound of that where it concerned Sloane and was sure she felt the same with him as her boyfriend. Where they went from there was anyone's guess. The one thing Gene knew for sure was he wanted Sloane to be a part of his life, be it as a steady romantic mate and best friend or possibly more down the line.

Gene was all smiles when the red Nissan Sentra drove up to the bed-and-breakfast. He stepped outside to welcome his hometown guests.

"If it isn't Mr. Bed-and-Breakfast himself," said Walter Griffin, grinning. "What's up, man?"

"Aloha," Gene offered the taller, wider man, giving him a big hug. He stepped back and studied his friend. "Do I detect a little gray in that closely cropped black hair?"

Walter squared his shoulders. "Maybe just a little. What can I say? That's what being a hotshot law professor does to you."

Gene laughed, running a hand over his shaved head. "The same might be true for a bed-and-breakfast owner if he had any hair." Smiling, he turned to Talia. She was small-boned and attractive with bold brown eyes, and her black hair was done up in a corkscrew-braid interlock. "Hey, Tal."

She grinned broadly. "Aloha, Gene."

"Aloha." He gave her a hug. "Good to see you again."

"You, too."

"How was the flight?" Gene asked her.

"Bumpy at times, smooth at others, and very long," she responded. "But the important thing is we made it here in one piece."

"There you have it," Gene agreed, and gave Walter a pat on the shoulder.

"Your house is huge," Talia proclaimed. "The brochure and pics you sent don't do it justice."

Gene grinned. "Let's go inside and I'll show you around."

"Sounds like a plan," Walter said. "And I can't wait to meet this lovely lady you've been going on about."

"She feels the same way," Gene said, knowing they would have to wait a little while longer to meet.

Sloane decided to take the afternoon off to hang out with Gene and his friends. She was sure it would mean a lot to Gene, and this would give her the opportunity to spend more time around him while in the company of people he cared about aside from his guests. She wasn't certain what to bring to his house, figuring that Gene likely had everything they would need as far as food and drink. In the end, Sloane settled on some gourmet chocolates and Maui Blanc pineapple wine.

She parked behind another car in the driveway of Malloy's Bed and Breakfast. After checking her hair, which was hanging loose as Gene had said he liked, and the little makeup she wore, Sloane emerged from the car. She still had on her work clothes of a gray ruffle-collar skirt suit and matching open-toe pumps. *Hope I'm not overdressed.*

She entered the house, hearing chatter and laughter. An older couple approached her wearing colorful matching Hawaiian shirts.

"Aloha," the man said. "I'm Roger Deeds and this is my wife Bonnie."

"Aloha," Sloane said to them with a smile. "I'm Sloane."

"Are you looking for Gene?" Bonnie asked.

"Yes."

"He's on the lanai out back with his friends."

"Thanks," Sloane said, and watched them go out the front door. She sucked in a deep breath and made her way through the house to the lanai, where she saw Gene and two people seated around a bistro table. "Aloha, everyone."

Gene beamed, immediately getting to his feet. "Sloane! I wasn't expecting you this early."

"I'm full of surprises," she said, trying to maintain her poise. "I wanted to come as soon as I could to meet your friends, so I came here right from work."

He gave her a quick peck on the lips. "I appreciate that," he said with a twinkle in his eye.

"I brought these," she said, handing him the chocolates and wine.

"Good choices, thanks." Then came the introductions as his guests stood. "This is my best friend, Walter Griffin, and his wife, Talia," said Gene. "Sloane Hepburn."

"Nice to meet you both." Sloane gave each of them a little hug as if they were old friends. Seemed like a nice way to break the ice, especially in Hawaii, where everyone was big on hugs over handshakes.

"Same here," Walter said, grinning. "Been hearing a lot about you."

"Oh…" Sloane glanced at Gene, realizing he had failed to ever bring up his friends until he told her they would be there in two days. She could only imagine what he had told Walter about her…them.

"All good, I promise." Gene chuckled unevenly as though reading her mind.

"He's telling you the truth." Walter backed him up. "Gene clearly thinks the world of you. Just as I do my baby." He gave Talia a nice kiss as if to prove his point.

"I think highly of him, too," Sloane said sweetly.

Talia brushed her hair away from her face. "I hear you're from Raleigh?"

Sloane met her eyes. "Yes."

"A girlfriend of mind teaches at North Carolina State University."

"Great school," Sloane said, and then proudly mentioned the University of North Carolina, where she attended college. She learned that Talia got her degree from the University of Michigan and Walter received a law degree from the University of Detroit Law School.

"Why don't I pop open this bottle of wine so we can all enjoy it?" Gene suggested.

"Good idea." Walter grinned. "I wouldn't mind sampling those chocolates, either."

Gene handed him the box. "Help yourself." He gazed at Sloane. "Do you want to get the wineglasses?"

"Sure, I'd be glad too," she said.

"Be right back," he told his friends. "Make yourselves right at home, as my place is yours for the next week."

Sloane followed him into the kitchen. "Since when did you need help with wineglasses?" she asked, batting her eyelashes.

Gene gave her a devilish smile. "Since the moment you stepped onto the lanai." He tucked his arms around Sloane's waist and pulled her closer. "The truth is I was just looking for an excuse to do this in private..." He bent his head down and kissed her liberally on the mouth.

Sloane kissed him back and found herself lost in the depths as their mouths joined, arousing her. She used all of her willpower to unlock their lips and slow down her heart rate. "Very enjoyable, but we shouldn't neglect your friends, who came all the way to Maui to see you."

"Not exactly." Gene wiped his mouth. "They're celebrating an anniversary and came to paradise for that. I just happen to have reasonably priced accommodations for their stay."

"They could have stayed at the Island Shores," Sloane pointed out. "I could've given them a great rate."

"You would have done that?"

"Of course. They're your friends, so naturally they would have gotten favorable treatment from me and the entire staff."

Gene grinned. "Better not tell them that," he kidded quietly. "Otherwise they might still be willing to jump ship."

Sloane chuckled. "I doubt that. I'm sure you will treat them like royalty, and they won't wish to be anywhere else."

"I know I don't wish to be anywhere else, so long as you're here," Gene said.

"Is that so?" He always seemed to find the right words to tug at her heart.

"Yeah, it is. So don't even think about moving to Oahu or some other island in the sun if another opportunity comes your way."

"And if I did, would you come after me?" she challenged him, knowing they were still getting used to being an official couple. Maybe this was where he drew the line.

Gene smiled crookedly. "I think I'd follow you to the end of the earth and back, if I had to. You mean that much to me."

Hearing Gene's words made Sloane feel even closer to him and made her believe that all things were possible within their relationship. But she wouldn't push it.

"In that case, good thing I am here to stay," she told him. "Wouldn't want you trekking across the planet and leaving your guests minus a host. Speaking of which, we'd better get back to Walter and Talia."

"I suppose you're right," he groaned.

"Now where are those glasses?"

"In that cabinet up there." He looked over her shoulder.

Sloane got the wineglasses and hoped to familiarize herself more with the surroundings, perhaps as a prelude to spending more time there in the future.

She cast her eyes at Gene affectionately. "Now let's show your friends from Detroit how to have a great time in Maui."

"I like the way you think," he said, grinning. "But then I like everything about you."

"Save that thought till later," she told him, anticipating the prospect of making love tonight just as she knew he was.

Chapter 9

The next day, Sloane took Talia shopping after Gene fixed a scrumptious breakfast. They went to some of the hottest boutiques and stores on the south side of the island that Sloane had wanted to check out. She came away with several business outfits, some running attire, and sexy lingerie that she was certain would turn Gene on. Talia was just as intent on spending money to make herself look great and impress her husband.

"We're going to be the hottest ladies in Maui," declared Talia as they left a shopping center with bags in hand.

"That we are," Sloane agreed. "Not to say we don't already fit the part."

Talia laughed. "Like two pieces of a beautiful puzzle in a beautiful place."

"Exactly." Sloane chuckled, feeling uplifted being with her.

Afterward, they went sightseeing, checking out some of

Maui's attractions such as Front Street in Lahaina, Makena Beach, and Iao Valley State Park before finishing with a stroll along Wailea Beach Walk.

"I can't believe you get to see all this every day of the year," Talia uttered, glancing at the ocean. "Must be nice."

"It *is* pretty cool," Sloane admitted, feeling at times as if she were in dreamland. "I haven't really gotten used to it yet."

"I doubt that I ever would."

"Maybe you guys should think about relocating," Sloane suggested. "There's always room for two more new residents in Maui."

"I wish," Talia said, her lashes fluttering with disappointment. "But Walter's tenure at the university and my job seniority make it hard to start over. I just don't see it happening. But that doesn't mean we can't come here more often now that we've taken the first big step."

"You should," Sloane said in a friendly voice. "There's plenty to see and do."

"I believe you, and I'm definitely envious." Talia looked at her. "So how did you and Gene meet?"

Sloane was surprised that he hadn't told the tale of his heroism. Obviously he'd downplayed the entire thing, which she commended him for, though it had seemed like a matter of life and death when the wave took her feet out from under.

"Wow, that's amazing and romantic at the same time," Talia said. "Especially with the beach and ocean as part of the equation, along with being in Maui."

Sloane laughed. "I guess so, when you put it that way. When I took a spill, I was just hoping I wasn't washed out into the ocean. Then Gene came along and made sure that didn't happen."

"And from that, a romance in paradise was made." Talia grinned.

"Well, let's just say it was the start of something," Sloane told her.

"It wasn't quite like that between me and Walter. We met at a film festival in Detroit. We both love movies and wanted to help support up-and-coming local filmmakers."

"How nice." Sloane slowed down, realizing she had slipped above the speed limit. Last thing she needed was a speeding ticket. "I didn't realize the film industry was a big thing in Detroit."

"It's not, but they're trying," Talia said. "Anyway, Walter and I hit it off, and a year and a half later we were married."

"What anniversary are you celebrating?"

"Lucky number ten, though it doesn't seem that long."

Sloane smiled. "Congratulations."

"Thanks."

"Any children?"

"Not yet," Talia answered. "We're working on that, figuring it's about time to start a family." She paused. "Have you ever been married?"

"No, I haven't." Sloane felt a little self-conscious in so saying, as if she were wearing a badge of shame by remaining single into her early thirties.

"Ever come close to marrying?"

"Honestly, I can't say I have," Sloane responded. "I've had boyfriends, but never anything very serious."

Talia raised a brow. "Was that by choice?"

"Yes, pretty much. I've always been career-oriented. I suppose I figured marriage and family might interfere with my career."

"Doesn't have to," Talia pointed out. "Walter and I have

great careers and still manage to have a great marriage at the same time."

"I can see that." Sloane grinned at her. "Maybe you really can have it all."

"Definitely, if that's what you want."

Sloane pointed out more attractions as they passed them and Talia was clearly in awe, just as Sloane had been when she first arrived. Her mind continued to wrap around the idea of marriage someday. Gene seemed like a good candidate should she ever choose to go down that road, except for the fact that his been there, done that approach made it seem like marriage might never be in the cards for them.

"What was Gene's ex-wife like?" she asked Talia impulsively, assuming they had known each other. *Am I really asking her this?*

"Well, she was high-maintenance, self-centered, spoiled, argumentative and hard to please," Talia answered bluntly.

Sloane laughed. "What were her good qualities?" Knowing Gene, she was sure he saw something redeeming, since he married the lady.

Talia chuckled. "For one, she fell in love with Gene and went after him. Lynda was also smart, attractive and charming when she wanted to be. Guess that was all Gene needed to be sold on her. At least for a while."

Long enough for them to move to Maui and open a bed-and-breakfast together, thought Sloane. Obviously that wasn't enough to hold things together.

"Why did they break up?" She'd gotten Gene's abbreviated side of the story. Maybe there was more to it.

Talia shifted in the seat. "I wasn't privy to all the dirty details, but from what I know, toward the end they were fighting on a regular basis over everything. Gene bent over backward to try and make it work, but the harder he tried, the more Lynda pushed him away. Things finally reached the point of no return and she left Gene."

"I'm sure he was devastated," Sloane stated sorrowfully.

"Relieved is more like it. I think deep down he knew it was only a matter of time." Talia sighed. "Though I can't prove this, I believe Lynda had someone else on the side when the relationship ended."

That was certainly an eye-opener to Sloane. "If that were true, then it was certainly better for Gene to move on."

"I absolutely agree with you," Talia said.

Sloane couldn't imagine ever wanting to be with another man if she were married to Gene, particularly with the attention he gave her in and out of the bedroom. Not to mention he had his act together as a successful businessman who wasn't afraid to go after his dreams. Or rescue damsels in distress when waves decided to target them for a bath. She wished his ex had not poisoned Gene against the idea of sharing that type of commitment with another woman.

"I'm so happy Gene met you," Talia's voice broke into Sloane's thoughts. "I know he's been busy running his business, but I think he's been lonely, even with the guests he sees day in and day out. You've taken away his loneliness."

"I'm happy we met, too," Sloane said. Gene never struck her as being lonely, but then she hadn't considered herself lonely either before they met. Now that Gene was in her system, Sloane was sure she'd be lost without him as an integral part of her life.

"I don't mean to jump the gun, but if you ever reach the point in your relationship where marriage comes up and you're open to the possibility, I hope you don't let Gene's failed marriage put you off. As far as I can tell, you're nothing like his ex."

Sloane smiled faintly. "Thanks for saying that. As for marriage, I doubt I'd be put off by Gene being divorced because I know it's part of his life. But I think he has a major problem with marrying again."

Talia's eyes widened. "He told you that?"

Sloane wondered if she should be sharing too much of their private discussions. She supposed she could trust Talia who, as the wife of Gene's best friend, seemed to have a grip on things.

"Yes, he made that pretty clear," she replied.

"That's not what he tells Walter, who then confides in me," Talia said.

"Oh..." Sloane regarded her. "And what exactly does he tell your husband?"

"That he's completely past Lynda and would like a second chance at love and marriage, if the right lady came his way."

"Really?" Sloane wondered if Gene was simply telling Walter as a married man what he wanted to hear. Or was Gene toying with her? *Maybe he doesn't consider me the right lady for marriage.*

"I think Gene's probably trying to protect himself against being hurt the way Lynda hurt him," Talia stated. "I'm sure he doesn't really mean marriage is out of the question. I know he likes you a lot, and if the opportunity came to put a ring on your finger, he'd do it in a heartbeat."

"That's interesting," Sloane said, not sure she bought into it. Maybe it was just wishful thinking on the part of Gene's friends to bring him into the married fold again. "As it is, Gene and I are far away from thinking in terms of marriage. Right now, we're still getting accustomed to being a couple as we juggle our respective careers. That might have to be enough as far as the future goes."

Or maybe the window is open for marriage in the future, if we continue to build our relationship and find we want to make it a permanent thing.

The next evening, Sloane had Gene and his friends over for dinner. She didn't make anything too fancy, going with steak, baked potatoes, corn and wheat bread. For dessert, she'd purchased a caramel cake. Drinks were lemonade and red wine.

"This is delicious," Walter told her as he ate.

Sloane smiled as she sliced into her steak. "Glad you like it."

He grinned and eyed Gene. "Maybe you should hire Sloane as your cook, old buddy. Yeah, I know you're not so bad in the kitchen and have Dayna to help out, but there's always room for improvement, right?"

Gene chuckled. "Can't argue with you there that Sloane knows her stuff. Unfortunately I doubt that I could pry her away from the Island Shores to feed my guests."

"Probably not, but it doesn't mean you can't hire her for part-time service."

Talia hit her husband on the shoulder. "Walter..."

He looked at her dumbfounded. "What did I say?"

"Just leave it alone. I'm sure if Sloane wanted to work at Gene's bed-and-breakfast, she would do so."

Sloane suddenly felt all eyes on her, prompting a response. "I appreciate the compliments on my cooking, but even if I wanted to, I'm nowhere near good enough to cook for Gene's guests. They come here expecting genuine Hawaiian cuisine. Not quite my specialty at the moment. Thanks, but I'm happy where I am and wouldn't want to take away Gene's business by pretending to be something I'm not."

"Well said," Gene said, meeting Sloane's eyes. "I couldn't agree more. That said, I came here as an outsider and learned all there was about the local culture and cuisine, so anyone can with time. Believe me, though, when I say I'm more than satisfied enjoying your cooking when I come here. Also, my breakfast menu is not exactly five-star food like they serve at the Island Shores, and my guests don't expect it to be. They only want to get off to a good start for the day and go from there."

Sloane liked how Gene stepped up and put the brakes to any attempts, well meaning as they were, by Walter to get her to play a role in the bed-and-breakfast. Not that she was opposed to helping out when she had the time, were Gene to ask. Right now, she was much more interested in spending private time with him in his house than being a servant for his guests.

"Would anyone like seconds?" she asked, smiling.

Following the meal, they went for a walk on the beach. Sloane and Gene lagged behind Walter and Talia, who were taking pictures of each other and the ocean, seeking to capture every moment of their anniversary trip.

"They're having a great time," Gene said, holding Sloane's hand. "Thanks in part to you."

Sloane blushed. She liked the feel of his hand covering hers. It made her feel they were truly a couple for the world to see.

"I've had fun with your friends," she told him. "Talia and I will definitely keep in touch."

"I'm sure she would like that."

"I also have a feeling this won't be the last time they come to Maui," Sloane said.

"I agree. Once you've gotten a taste of this place, it

becomes addictive." He kissed her cheek. "Just like I'm addicted to you."

Sloane squeezed his fingers. "I like the way that sounds."

"You'll like it even better when I put the words into practice tonight," he said sinfully.

"Hmm. Just what type of practice are we talking about?" she teased him.

"The type that has me exploring each and every part of your body—making every fiber in you beg me to be deep inside."

Sloane felt a prickle of heat between her legs. "Are you trying to get me wet in public?"

Gene's mouth curved up at the corners. "Maybe I am getting you ready early so that I have plenty of licking to look forward to."

She gazed up at him desirously. "You can lick to your heart's content."

"Just my heart?"

"And everything else you've got." She couldn't believe they were talking like this outside.

"I'll consider that a challenge," Gene said. "I promise I won't disappoint."

"You never do," Sloane conceded, at least where it came to sex. The jury was still out as far as other aspects of a relationship that they were working on.

"Neither do you," he told her, putting his arm around her and planting a succulent kiss on her lips.

Sloane pulled one of his lips into her mouth, unabashedly savoring the taste of him before Talia and Walter came upon them.

"Get a room," Talia joked.

Sloane touched her mouth. "We already have one. Make that two."

"And so do we." Talia giggled. "Guess we'd all better get to them and see what trouble we can stir up."

Walter held her slender waist from behind. "It's never any trouble as far as I'm concerned."

Gene laughed, hugging Sloane. "You've got that right. No trouble at all."

Sloane colored, though feeling surprisingly comfortable with Gene's friends and the intimate talk. She knew Gene could definitely walk the walk, as could she. It made the buildup that much more rewarding.

"Sloane is definitely a keeper," Walter told Gene later that night as the two sat on the lanai drinking beers.

Gene lifted his bottle. "You think so?"

"Don't know the lady very well, but from what I see and what Talia tells me, you two seem meant for each other."

Gene did not disagree. How could he when he felt the same way? "Maybe we are," he said. "We haven't gotten around to finishing each other's sentences yet, but I do feel pretty damned good about being in her company."

"There's certainly some natural chemistry between you two that I never saw with you and Lynda," Walter told him.

Gene recalled the sexual chemistry that had the sheets burning when he was inside Sloane an hour ago. "Maybe because what Lynda and I had was never real. At least it seems that way right now."

Walter peered at him. "And you think it's real, what you feel for Sloane, and vice versa?"

"Yeah, we definitely click."

"You mean like love?"

Gene pondered the question. Was it love? Lust? Both? "It's getting there," he said without commitment, fearful of jinxing what they had.

"And by the look of things, like the way you two were all over each other on the beach, I'd say the 'getting there' feelings are mutual."

Gene gulped down a swig of beer. Was Sloane falling in love with him? If so, what was she looking for out of this relationship? Could he give it to her?

"We'll see where it goes," he said. "I don't want to mess this up or get too excited about us only to have it all fall apart."

"You can't think that way, man," Walter insisted. "You won't mess anything up as long as you be yourself and be straight with Sloane. As far as excitement, you're entitled to get excited about having a beauty like Sloane in your life after being on your own for way too long."

"Yeah, I know." He acknowledged that it felt like it had been forever being without companionship after his divorce. Now Gene could hardly imagine not having someone like Sloane in his life.

"Maybe Talia and I will be back here for a wedding," suggested Walter.

Gene looked at him defensively. "Now wait a minute, no one said anything about wedding bells."

Walter chuckled. "Chill, man. That's just me talking. But now that I put it out there, don't close your mind to the idea. I seem to recall you told me that you wanted a second opportunity to get things right. Maybe this is it."

"I'm not saying it isn't," Gene voiced thoughtfully, realizing he and Sloane had broached the subject uneasily. They had decided to leave it alone for a later day when there was more reason to delve into it. "Sloane and I will take things as they come," Gene told him.

Walter leaned forward. "I don't want to push this, but I think you and Sloane could do a hell of a good job running this bed-and-breakfast together. Yeah, I know she's got her gig at the posh resort hotel, but with her knowledge of pleasing folks and your operational acumen, it just sounds like an arrangement that could be ideal both personally and professionally."

"Maybe," Gene allowed, "except for one thing—Sloane has her job, probably making damned good money. Surely more than I could ever pay her. Asking her to give that up sounds crazy." He also wondered how it would work if they were living apart. Would Sloane feel crowded were they to share his quarters in a bed-and-breakfast?

"Not if it were for reasons of the heart. People do crazy things for love." Walter tilted his head. "Or have you forgotten how that feels?"

Gene hadn't forgotten the feeling, only the person he'd shared such emotion with. Now Sloane was in his life and he was still grappling with the feelings he had for her and where those feelings could lead in their romance.

Sloane was awakened when she felt the tenderness of Gene's tongue between her legs arousing her. She cradled his head in her hands and pressed down, not wanting him to stop what he was doing in pleasuring her. Fortunately, he seemed perfectly content to accommodate her silent wishes. She bit down on her lower lip and rode the wave of sexual ecstasy coursing through her veins.

When the need to come overpowered her, Sloane fought back the urge, wanting Gene to be inside her when she had an orgasm. She gently coaxed him out from between her thighs so she could see his face.

"I want us to come together," she whispered in a plea. "Make love to me now."

Gene sucked in a deep breath and put on a condom before he spread Sloane's legs wide and entered her. She made sure he went as deep as possible by arching her back and giving in to his penis, drawing it inside with her contractions. He cupped her buttocks and propelled himself even deeper while their mouths kissed desperately.

Sloane clawed at his back as Gene's powerful thrusts brought her to a new level of satisfaction, the effect causing her heart to pound rapidly. She soaked in the scent of their perspiring bodies wrapped in intercourse and tasted Gene's tongue as he breathed raggedly into her mouth. She jumped when his body began to shake passionately as his surge emptied out of him, then held Gene tightly as her own climax erupted like thunder and lightning.

Sloane gasped sharply from the onslaught of their frenetic lovemaking that peaked for a full minute of sexual intensity before their bodies began to relax and their breathing returned to normal. Gene rested his head on her breasts, and they lay there too exhausted to speak right away.

Finally, Sloane cooed, "Hope you knew what you were getting into when you decided to wake me up."

"I had a good feeling how things might end up," he said coolly and licked her nipple.

"Male intuition, was it?" she asked, licking her lips.

"More like I knew you wanted me every bit as much as I wanted you. It was just a matter of bringing your body back to life and letting the rest take care of itself."

She smiled with satisfaction. "I'd say you accomplished your objective pretty well."

He looked into her sable eyes. "Any accomplishments came together. I wouldn't want it any other way."

"Neither would I," Sloane murmured, reaching up to kiss his mouth solidly, leaving her wanting more.

Chapter 10

A week later, Sloane was at work performing her duties as guest relations director, wondering if it was truly enough to satisfy her. She loved her job. Or at least she thought she did. But now Gene had opened her eyes to more possibilities in Maui. She was no longer content merely moving up the career ladder with little need for a man in her life. Now she wanted so much more, like coming home to someone every day and waking up to that person every morning.

Someone like Gene Malloy would fit the bill nicely. She sensed that he might want this, too. But how they would make this work was still up for debate. What she wanted most was to love and be loved as the centerpiece of any relationship. If that could lead to marriage, all the better.

Am I really saying I want to get married at this stage of my life?

Sloane was shocked at just how much her view of things had changed in a relatively short time. What did it mean exactly? Was it merely a passing phase or was it something that would forever have a profound impact on her life and where she went with it from here?

She greeted more guests with leis and spotted a family that she had directed to the Sugar Cane Train the day before.

"Aloha," Sloane said to them with a bright smile. "Were you able to take a ride on the train?"

"Yes, we sure were and really enjoyed it," responded the father, a blonde-haired man in his thirties.

"Yeah, it was so cool," remarked his preteen son.

"I'm glad to hear that," Sloane said.

"Afterward, we went to the Kahana Pond Waterfowl Sanctuary," remarked the wife, her short black hair parted in the middle. "I've always wanted to visit it and see some endangered Hawaiian species like stilt and coot."

Sloane smiled at her. "Sounds like you're having a great time."

"We are," she said. "You've been a big help."

"Mahalo," Sloane replied, and then took the opportunity to recommend that they visit the Maui Tropical Plantation, certain the family would find it entertaining.

A few minutes later, Sloane stepped outside for a brief respite. It had rained periodically the past two days, but now the sun had come out and there wasn't a cloud in the sky. She took out her cell phone and returned the call from her friend Gail Littleton.

"Hey, Gail. Sorry I didn't get back to you sooner. It's been crazy around here."

"It's okay," Gail said. "I know the feeling. Been a madhouse here, too."

"So what's up?" Sloane asked.

"I just broke up with my boyfriend."

Sloane cocked a brow. "I didn't know you were involved with anyone in particular."

"I started seeing him before you left, but didn't say anything till I knew if something would come of it."

"Sorry it didn't work out with him," Sloane told her and thought about her own relationship with Gene and its long-term potential.

"I'm not," muttered Gail. "Turned out he was still hung up on his last girlfriend and I wasn't about to compete with anyone, so I showed him the door. But it still hurts anyhow."

"You did the right thing. You don't need someone like that."

"I know." Gail paused. "So how are things with you and Gene?"

"Good," Sloane told her. "We've been having a nice time together when we find the time to spend with each other."

"So he's the real deal?"

Sloane waved at two guests passing by. "Yes, I think he is," she responded thoughtfully. "So far, so good."

"I'm happy for you," Gail said. "He doesn't happen to have a brother he could hook me up with, does he?"

"To tell you the truth, I don't know," admitted Sloane, realizing there was still more to learn about Gene Malloy. "I can always ask."

"You do that. In the meantime, I'll be fine with work keeping me plenty busy."

"Just don't get too caught up in the job," Sloane warned her, though Gail had a great thing going with her own business, selling antiques and collectibles. "That can't keep you warm at night."

"Look who's talking." Gail giggled. "I've been telling you the same thing for years."

Sloane laughed. "I know. Well, things have changed, and I realize the job can only carry you so far in life."

"Isn't that the truth," Gail agreed. "I'm glad you're beginning to realize it now that you've got Gene as a welcome distraction."

And what a distraction he was, Sloane thought wistfully. The man was damned hard to forget. Especially when he was up close and personal or they were ripping each other's clothes off and leaving nothing to the imagination.

"Talk to you soon." Gail slipped into her thoughts. "Enjoy the rest of your day."

"You, too," Sloane said, disconnecting the phone.

She was about to head back inside when she looked up into Gene's handsome face.

"Hi," he said in his resonant voice as he removed his sunglasses.

"Hey." She met his gaze. "Where did you come from?"

"Your dreams," he teased.

Sloane knew there was some merit to his words, but didn't want to inflate his ego any more than it already was. "You wish."

His mouth parted seductively. "I'm always wishing for more and more where you're concerned."

"Oh, really?" She batted her eyes flirtatiously. "You're never satisfied, are you?"

Gene's eyes gleamed. "Sometimes I am, until the need hits me again."

Sloane's face flushed. She couldn't believe they were practically jumping each other's bones in broad daylight. At least the steamy words implied as much. Though it was arousing, she couldn't let the situation get out of hand while she was working.

"That's enough," she scolded him.

He laughed. "I promise I'll be on my best behavior for now."

"Good." She gave him a doubtful look. "Well, I have to get back to work."

"I won't keep you," he said. "I just stopped by to see if you would like to go on a little trip with me this weekend."

Sloane's eyes widened. "Where to?"

"Hana. I have some friends with a bed-and-breakfast there. I usually go up at least once a year and they come down here."

"Hmm. I've heard the drive to Hana is pretty dangerous."

"I won't lie, it can be kind of scary at times," Gene admitted. "But that's half the fun of the Hana experience. Besides, once you get there and see how stunning and peaceful it is, you will definitely feel the end more than justifies the means. Not to mention you'll be with me and I won't let anything happen to you that you don't want to happen." He eyed her with a crooked smile. "So what do you say?"

Sloane conceded that his charming way with words along with his strong masculine sexual appeal made it hard for her to say no. But there was still the matter of work.

"I'm supposed to work this weekend," she told him. "But…I suppose I can get someone to sub for me, if I ask hard enough."

Gene's cheeks dimpled. "Cool. I'll let my friend know we're coming. You'll have a great time, I promise."

She had little doubt about that. Not when she would be in the company of the man who made her heart flutter with just a simple facial expression, let alone when he put extra effort into capturing her attention or pleasuring her in one respect or another.

Just as Gene was starting to leave, Sloane called out to him. “By the way, you don’t happen to have a brother, do you?”

He grinned. “No, afraid not. Why do you ask?”

She thought about Gail and her desire to find a man like Gene to romance. Clearly he was one of a kind. And Sloane aimed to keep him as hers.

“No reason,” she told him pensively.

“Don’t worry about anything,” Dayna Yee told Gene as he stood at the front door ready to head out to Hana. “Your place will be in good hands.”

“I have no doubt about that,” he said, smiling. “But just in case you need me for anything, you have my cell number.”

“And even the number to the bed-and-breakfast where you’ll be staying at in Hana.” Dayna winked at him. “Now go and have a great time with your pretty lady.”

“That I will.” Gene gave her a kiss on the cheek and stepped outside. He spoke for a couple of minutes with two of his guests, who were on their way to the Maui Nui Botanical Gardens, before heading to his car.

Gene drove to Sloane’s place, excited that she was accompanying him on the picturesque, heart-pounding journey to Hana. He considered it a good bonding experience for them away from their familiar surroundings and comfort zone. It also showed him that Sloane was up for a challenge and willing to rearrange her schedule to accommodate his request.

She was outside waiting when he approached the condominium.

“Hi.” Sloane flashed him a terrific smile.

Gene took one look at her in a red puff-sleeve scoop-neck top and jean shorts, her sexy legs bare down to her sneakers, and felt aroused. *She's smokin' hot.* He forced himself to contain his libido, but knew it was only a temporary thing that she was able to reawaken anytime.

He gave her a kiss. "You look great."

"What else is new?" she asked jokingly.

"You're right, it does go without saying."

"But feel free to say it anyway, anytime you like."

"I will." Gene grinned. "All set?"

"Ready, set and here we come," Sloane said with a chuckle, a bag strapped across her shoulder.

They were soon on the Hana Highway. Having been there twice before, Gene braced himself for the nerve-rattling ride.

"How long does it take to get to Hana?" Sloane asked.

"Well, it's only around fifty miles or so," Gene answered with deliberation. "But because of the narrow, winding road, traffic and fifty-nine bridges, forty-six of which are only one lane, it could be anywhere from two to four hours. Probably closer to four hours."

Sloane chuckled nervously. "Wow. Guess I'd better hang on for the ride."

Gene grinned, noting she had her seat belt on securely. "You'll survive. That's not to say you won't get that roller-coaster feeling every now and then. But that's all part of the Hana experience."

She wrinkled her nose. "If you say so."

He cut on some soul music and watched as Sloane began to bob her head to the beat and relax. That was a good first step in their adventure.

"Why did you wonder if I had a brother?" he asked curiously.

"Oh, that. My friend Gail is having some man troubles right now, so she wondered if there was a genetic clone of you somewhere."

Gene blushed. "Sorry, there's only one of me in this world. And he belongs only to you."

"Nice to know." She grinned. "I told her she'll have to find her own Mr. Right."

"So I'm your Mr. Right, huh?"

She gave him a straight look. "You're okay, so far. We'll see if that holds up over time."

He grinned. "I'll do my best to measure up to that lofty image."

Sloane gazed down at his crotch. "Um, I'd say you measure up just fine."

Gene laughed while imagining them on the beach making love. "I'll remember that."

Just then he made a hairpin turn on the narrow, curving road and quickly corrected himself, aware there was a steep drop below to a deep gorge should he lose control of the vehicle.

"Whew!" Sloane glared at him. "That was close. I hope you know what the hell you're doing."

Gene glanced her way with a half smile. "Yeah, I'm on top of it. I promise that not one hair on that gorgeous head will be hurt."

She sighed. "Right. I'll believe that when we get there… and back."

"Would I lie?" He chuckled.

"That remains to be seen. Just please keep your eyes on the road and both hands on the steering wheel."

"Will do." He resisted the urge to touch her. "You know, it's sexy when you get riled up like that."

"You would think that," she snorted. "And I'm not riled up. Just scared, that's all."

"Don't worry," Gene said, "the best is yet to come."

"I'm not sure that's very comforting."

"Trust me. It will be."

Gene had to negotiate another spine-tingling turn, but managed to do so without scaring Sloane too much. Soon he had gotten into a groove and she began to better appreciate what he'd been talking about. They saw scenic views of the northern coastline, plummeting seaside cliffs, black-sand beaches, coastal rain forests, amazing waterfalls and lush, tropical vegetation. They stopped at several lookouts, and Sloane took pictures galore. This in and of itself made the trip worthwhile for Gene, just to see Sloane in her element and eager to take in more and more.

Sloane breathed in the organic scent of the rain forests, utterly amazed at the exquisite scenery she was witnessing. At first she'd been beginning to question the wisdom of putting her life on the line with the harrowing twists and turns on the road to Hana. Now she was happy to have the opportunity to experience for herself what she'd heard others talk about for so long.

She took more pictures with her digital camera as they stood in a spot that offered marvelous views of guava fruit trees and very old waterfalls carved through fern and rock.

"Wow is all I can say," Sloane said.

"I think everyone is wowed by this," Gene said, amused. "Does it get any more beautiful?"

"Not from where I'm standing." She clicked a picture of him in a Maui T-shirt and blue shorts that accentuated his sexy muscled arms and legs. She found Gene every bit as appealing to her senses as the ideal creation of a man as the nature surrounding them.

Gene showed his teeth, making him all the more handsome and photogenic. "That's enough of me," he said, stepping aside. "Focus more on everything around us."

"If you insist." Sloane took one more picture of him and then resumed pointing the camera elsewhere.

They got back on the road and braved several more dangerous curves, nail-biting turns and shaky bridges high above tumbling waterfalls and coastal valleys that made Sloane hold her breath, though she was still confident in Gene's ability to handle the driving. Finally, they arrived in Hana.

"Aloha!" Sloane sang.

"Aloha," Gene echoed and broke into a hearty laugh. "That wasn't really so bad, was it?"

She chuckled. "I'll take the Fifth on that one."

"Well, we're here now and can start a whole new part of the adventure."

"I can hardly wait," she said, regarding his profile and imagining that some of their adventure would be spent in bed, all over each other.

They pulled into the lot at Hana's Sunrise Bed and Breakfast. It was a two-story country Victorian that was larger than Gene's B&B and set on a couple of acres amidst bamboo trees with sweeping views of the ocean and mountains. Sloane was awed and eager to see inside.

"Your friends have a gorgeous bed-and-breakfast," she told Gene.

"Yeah, they've got a great property here," he agreed. "Makes for a perfect getaway for anyone who's daring enough to brave the trip here."

They went inside and were greeted by the hosts, who hugged Gene and kissed him on both cheeks.

"This is Aiko and Kehau Poaipuni," Gene introduced.

Sloane smiled at the sixtysomething Samoan couple. "Sloane Hepburn." She was also kissed on both cheeks by them.

"You were right, Gene," Aiko said with an eye on Sloane. "Your lady friend is quite stunning."

"Mahalo," Sloane said, blushing.

"And genial, too." He laughed warmly. "Nice of you to visit our part of the island."

"Gene made it sound irresistible." Sloane smiled at him. "And from everything I've seen thus far, he was right."

"Hey, all I did was speak the truth," Gene said. "The rest you can blame on nature, along with such heartwarming folks as Aiko and Kehau."

Kehau giggled. "Always the charmer, Gene. We do our best to keep up the traditions of Hana." She cupped her arm under Sloane's. "Why don't we show you to your room so you can freshen up?"

"Sounds good," Sloane told her, certain the room would reflect everything else she'd seen of the place. Moreover, she wanted to see where she and Gene would be spending some private time on this side of the island.

The Ku'uipo Suite did not disappoint. Upstairs, it had a private lanai and offered a panoramic view of the ocean and two other islands.

"I love it!" Sloane declared.

"So do I," Gene said, and thanked their hosts again.

"Always the best for you and yours, Gene," Aiko said. "Expect the same the next time you visit my place."

"Of course."

When they left, Gene put his arms around Sloane's waist. "So here we are."

"Yes." She raised her eyes to meet his. "We made it."

"Glad you came?"

Sloane fluttered her lashes seductively. "That will depend on how well we make the most of our time here."

A slow grin spread across Gene's mouth. "Oh, I'm

sure we will take full advantage of the setting…and each other."

"Hmm…" Her eyes closed as she imagined putting the words into heated action.

Gene kissed her, parting Sloane's lips and sliding his tongue inside. The kiss left Sloane light on her feet while heavy in her need for this man. But she fought back the urge, realizing they would have two nights to explore each other and more.

She pulled their mouths apart. "That's a good start. I'll expect you to finish it a little later."

He licked his lips. "Without a doubt. You've got my word on that."

"I'll need more than just your word to back that up." Sloane glanced at his trousers, detecting the bulge that clearly wanted only to be inside her.

"And you'll have it," Gene said with assurance, leaving Sloane hot with anticipation.

They met the other guests and mingled in the downstairs living room while the Poaipunis served apple muffins, fresh island fruit and tropical juices. Gene was glad to see that Sloane fit right in, just as she did at his bed-and-breakfast, engaging others without being prompted and comfortable in her own shoes. It was but one reason why he liked her so much. She was as down-to-earth as he was and not afraid to take chances and accept new challenges. He suspected this was what had drawn her to Maui in the first place. And into his arms and bed. He saw no reason why they shouldn't continue to bask in each other's company with no end in sight.

That afternoon, Gene took Sloane to the Hana Cultural Center and Museum. There they saw the Kauhale O Hana, an authentic recreation complex of housing and gardens that reflected life prior to European contact.

"That's very interesting," Sloane said, holding Gene's hand as they walked through the museum.

"I thought so too, the first time I visited," he told her.

"I'll certainly take mental notes on everything we see here so I can recommend it to guests at the Island Shores."

"Good idea. Call it firsthand research, which is the same thing I do when I come to Hana and steer others in this direction."

Sloane looked at him curiously. "So this was like half a business trip for you?"

Gene lowered his eyes to meet hers. "Not at all. I wanted us to experience this magnificent place together. Anything else is strictly incidental."

"Perfect answer," she told him, flashing her teeth.

He smiled. "That's what you've done to me. My focus these days is almost entirely on you."

"I could say the same thing. Wonder what it means?"

Gene gave her a thoughtful gaze. "Guess it means we've found something special."

"I like being special to someone," Sloane said softly.

"As you should. And I like being with you."

She lifted her chin and kissed his mouth, then wiped his lips with her pinkie. "How about we go back to our room and make good use of the bed?"

"You read my thoughts," Gene said, feeling aroused. Or was it the other way around?

After some heated sex and exchanging needy kisses to complete the shared seduction, Sloane lay naked in Gene's protective arms, her head resting comfortably on his chest. She found herself wondering how he felt about various things in life as part of getting to know him on a broader level and seeing how they stacked up to one another.

"I have some questions for you," she said, angling her eyes up at him.

"Do you now?" His voice lowered a notch with curiosity. "Ask away."

"What were you like as a boy?"

"Oh, pretty much the same as I am now—fun-loving, witty, adventurous, insightful and always wanting to look at what's in front of me rather than behind."

"When did you have your first crush?" Sloane asked.

"When I was eight. I thought my teacher, Ms. Bellwood, was hot."

Sloane chuckled. "Did you ever cheat in college?"

"Not once," Gene responded with a straight face. "I didn't want to shortchange my education or future."

"Good for you." She paused. "Who do you most admire, not including your parents?"

"I'd say Barack Obama, with Nelson Mandela a close second."

"Nice answers." Sloane nodded. "Do you believe in God?"

"Yes."

"Do you believe in extraterrestrial life?"

Gene laughed. "You really are darting all over the map, aren't you?"

"What better way to dig deeper into the man?" Sloane asked.

"I can go along with that. Yes, I believe that there are probably other life forms outside this planet. Why should we be all alone in the cosmos?"

Sloane was enjoying this, especially since their answers were similar for the questions up to this point.

"What's your favorite sports team?" she asked.

"The New Orleans Saints," he said, "followed by the Houston Rockets."

"I didn't hear a Detroit team there."

He gave a wry chuckle. "Exactly."

She chuckled as well. "Have you ever traced your roots?"

"Good question." Gene ran his hand along her shoulder. "No, I haven't, but I'd love to do it and see where it leads."

Sloane was also very interested in tracing her roots. She knew painfully little about her ancestry and hoped to learn more in time.

"What's your favorite movie?" she asked, enjoying the feel of his fingers caressing her arm.

"*Titanic,* maybe. Or *Star Wars.*"

"I loved the first Harry Potter movie," noted Sloane, "but I probably like *The Sound of Music* best. I'm a sucker for musicals and sentimental tales."

He nodded, thoughtful. "Yeah, I can see that."

"So when was your first sexual experience?" Sloane had not intended to ask this, as the last thing she wanted was to be compared with any woman he may have bedded, including his ex. But she threw it out anyway, just to see what he would say.

"Where did that come from?" Gene asked.

"Nowhere in particular," she told him. "Just wondered."

"I was sixteen. She lived down the street. It wasn't very memorable."

Sloane ran her foot across his leg, slipping it between his legs. "How about your current sexual experience? Memorable?"

Gene groaned lustfully. "Very unforgettable."

She licked his nipple and saw it rise. "Glad to hear that I'm embedded in your mind."

"You're embedded in more than just my mind," he uttered, a lascivious edge to his tone.

"Oh really?" Sloane looked at him longingly. "Maybe we can work on building those memories a little more."

Gene put his hand between her legs, feeling her arousal. "One body part at a time…"

Chapter 11

The next day, Sloane and Gene spent time on the black-sand beach of Hana's Waianapanapa State Park. Once again, Sloane was fascinated by the view, along with the Hawaiian legend regarding freshwater caves. She took her fair share of pictures and planned to have an online photo album to display.

They went from there to tour the Ka'eleku Caverns, winding underground lava-tube trails that had gone unchanged for 30,000 years. They followed that with a visit to Kahanu Garden, located in one of the Hawaiian Islands' largest untamed native hala forests. It was home to a variety of ethnobotanical plants, particularly those of the Pacific Islands.

"I'd love to have some of these plants in my garden, if I had one," remarked Sloane, feeling warm and cozy with Gene's arm around her.

"In fact, I have a couple of them at the bed-and-breakfast," he told her. "They're not always that easy to manage, but wonderful to look at."

"I know what you mean." Sloane recalled her garden when she lived in Raleigh. It could at times be a bear to tend to, yet the end result always proved more than worthwhile.

"Don't tell me you have a green thumb?"

She raised her eyes. "Is that so surprising?"

He chuckled. "Nothing about you surprises me."

"Nothing at all?" she challenged him.

"Well, maybe I'm still a little surprised that such a lovely, smart, well-rounded lady like yourself should wind up in Maui without a man in her life. But that's a good thing, from where I stand."

Sloane regarded him boldly. "Could be that I was simply biding my time till the right man came along," she said.

Gene snuggled her a bit closer. "And did he?"

She felt his warm breath on her cheek. "You tell me."

"I'd say you found precisely the right man to be in your life."

"Oh, you think so, do you?" Sloane teased.

"Yeah, I certainly do."

He tilted her face and brought their lips together. The kiss was just long enough to get Sloane's heart racing before Gene moved his mouth away.

"I'd have to agree with you," she told him with a sigh.

He beamed. "I thought you might see things my way."

"You make it hard not to," Sloane admitted. And it was getting harder with each day to not want to spend it with him. Part of her wished they could just retire from life and devote every waking moment to making each other happy. If only. The reality was they had responsibilities that neither could walk away from. But that didn't mean she couldn't dream of having the man all to herself.

* * *

After they had dinner with the Poaipunis and the other guests, Gene whisked Sloane away for what he said was a surprise. Her curiosity was more than a little piqued, wondering what else he had up his sleeve.

"What is this?" she asked after he drove her to the beach.

"Not just another beach," Gene said mysteriously. "Kaihalulu Beach is a sight to behold with its red cinder beach and lagoons."

"You've got my attention."

"Don't I always?" He grinned sideways. "C'mon, let's take a walk. I want you to see something."

She could read the slow seduction in his dark eyes, beguiling her. "All right."

After they removed their shoes, Gene took Sloane's hand as they walked down the beach near the shoreline. The sun was slowly beginning to set and the water glistened from its rays.

"Aren't you afraid a sneaker wave might come and sweep us away?" Sloane asked nervously.

Gene laughed. "Not a chance. I won't let one catch us off guard. Besides, I've got other plans that don't include being washed out to sea."

"Hmm...wonder what those might be?" Her eyes darted up to his face.

"Oh, just a nice way to make our last night in Hana memorable."

"You mean create our own memories?"

He grinned slyly. "Something like that."

They padded across the sand away from the water and onto a secluded beach.

"What do you think?" Gene asked.

"It's amazing," Sloane responded, noting the sand was pristine. "How did you find this?"

"The Poaipunis showed it to me last year. Most visitors overlook it, settling for the more popular spots on the beach."

"Their misfortune."

Gene put his hands on Sloane's shoulders. "Ever made love on the beach?"

"Never," she answered without prelude.

"Why don't we do something about that?"

She met his eyes. "Such as?"

"Such as this." Gene cupped her cheeks and kissed her mouth. "And this..." He ran his fingers torturously across her nipples. "And this." He took her hand and placed it on the bulge in his pants. "I want you."

Sloane gasped as she pictured his throbbing erection inside of her. "I think you've got me."

Gene kissed her again. "Oh, I know I have you whenever I want. And that's now."

They sank down onto the sand, which felt to Sloane like a warm, soft mattress with no borders. She watched Gene inch her dress up over her thighs and then put his face between her legs. She felt his teeth nudge aside her thong, giving him unencumbered access to her private parts.

Sloane shuddered violently as Gene licked her clitoris relentlessly while holding her thighs to keep them in place. Though she wanted nothing more than for him to be deep inside her body for her first beach orgasm, the sensations were too intense, too pleasing, too deliberate to be able to contain herself. Sloane swung her head left and right, moaning louder than she wanted to as the moment of ecstasy erupted between her legs and quickly spread in waves throughout her body.

When Gene had finished what he clearly wished to have happen, he lifted his head. "Did you enjoy that?"

"Do you have to ask?" Sloane was still trying to re-establish her equilibrium.

He grinned ravenously. "No, your quivering body, the way you got so very wet every time I licked you, told me everything I needed to know."

"Not everything," she told him desirously. "I was still holding back until your penis impaled me over and over again. Please don't make me wait a moment longer. Otherwise I'll scream."

"Go ahead," he said. "No one will hear but me. And I like the sounds of your lust."

Unzipping his pants, Gene pulled out his erect penis and rapidly slipped on a condom. He sank to his knees into the sand between Sloane's propped-up legs. He burrowed into her with such need that Sloane winced from the sheer quickness of his manhood filling her. She quickly adjusted, giving in to him to allow deeper entry. He pinned Sloane's arms over her head, then brought his mouth down hard upon hers. She tasted herself on his lips and tongue penetrating her mouth, arousing Sloane that much more while Gene plunged into her over and over, bringing her to a new high.

Their bodies and clothes were slick with sweat and covered with sand while they lay there locked in passionate lovemaking, each arousing the other with kisses, touches, nibbles, scents, pounding heartbeats and finally cries as they were caught in the throes of orgasmic release. Sloane clung to Gene's hard body and screamed out his name as they came together in one earth-moving moment of satisfaction.

Afterwards, a deep sigh and chuckle escaped Gene's

lips. "We may have to escape to the beach more often for some fun in the sun."

Sloane breathed in the erotic redolence of their sex. "I'm game, if you are."

"Yeah, I am game anytime," he promised.

"Good. In the meantime, just kiss me again."

"With pleasure."

Sloane widened her mouth, embracing Gene's as it contoured with hers. She explored the soft and tasty inside of his lips with her tongue and teeth, and wrapped her arms around his neck. She loved kissing him and could do so all day, enjoying the movement of his mouth on hers, using his tongue at just the right times and places.

In that moment of clarity, it became abundantly clear to Sloane what she had not admitted to herself till now. She had started to fall in love with Gene Malloy. She wondered if the feeling was mutual.

On Monday, Sloane was back at work, her fascinating trip to Hana still fresh on her mind. How could it not be, when she could still taste and smell Gene as they found new ways to merge sexually? It also brought about a new awareness of her feelings for the man, though she was unsure what it meant for their relationship or its future.

She was at her desk when Kendra came up to it, gazing at Sloane with what she perceived to be a snooping look. "Well?"

"Well, what?" Sloane rolled her eyes, playing dumb.

"How was the big weekend in Hana? Or shouldn't I ask?"

"You can ask. It was fabulous." Sloane satisfied her curiosity with a summary of the trip, including some hot romance with Gene.

"Is there anything that your man doesn't do?" Kendra batted her lashes outrageously.

"Hmm..." Sloane flashed a dreamy smile. "Not that I can think of."

"I am so jealous. I've got to get Edy to take me to Hana and make more sparks fly."

"Go for it." Sloane looked at her. "In fact, I intend to recommend it to everyone who seems adventurous."

"Just how adventurous does one have to be?" Kendra asked nervously.

Sloane laughed. "Only enough to hang on to your seat with your eyes closed every now and then on the drive there. But trust me, it's worth the trip."

"So I hear. And now that you've gone, I have to be brave and try it too."

"You won't regret it," Sloane assured her. "Especially with Edy to keep you occupied."

They both turned as Alan Komoda approached them. He gave Kendra a cursory nod and focused on Sloane. "Got a minute?"

"Sure." Sloane eyed Kendra, who understood it was her time to depart.

"Better get back to it," she said. "See you later."

After Kendra had left them alone, Sloane wondered what was on Alan's mind. Maybe some big client was coming in who needed special attention.

"Seems like two of our guests, Russell and Penny Delacorte, are planning to check out prematurely." Alan frowned. "Something about having a change of heart with their accommodations."

"Oh, boy," Sloane said, wondering how anyone could have a change of heart about staying at the fabulous Island Shores.

"As you know, we try to keep our guests and the money

they spend in-house for as long as they're in Maui," Alan stressed.

Sloane sensed what was expected of her. "Maybe I can talk to them to see if there's a problem we can straighten out."

"Good idea. People don't just leave a resort hotel without a reasonable explanation."

"I agree." Sloane took a breath. "I'll get to the bottom of it."

"Hope so." Alan gave her an optimistic look. "Also, we have a large group coming in next week from St. Louis for a corporate event. Apparently the spouses were invited, and many are expected to attend. They've requested that we find ways to keep them occupied for several days apart from the norm of hanging out on the beach, shopping, and dining."

A smile formed on Sloane's lips. "I'm sure I can come up with any number of exciting things for the spouses to do." She assumed most were female, but would make arrangements that were gender neutral to account for male spouses too. "The more I've come to know the island, the more possibilities I see for our guests during their stay."

Alan grinned crookedly. "Glad to know that you're taking stock of your surroundings and applying it to your position as guest director."

"The two go hand in hand as far as I'm concerned," she stressed.

"Keep me posted. And best of luck with the Delacortes."

Sloane wasn't sure if she would need luck or not. In her experience, there were two types of disgruntled guests. Those who were flexible and leveraged this to get a room upgrade or other perks. Then there were the guests who were obstinate in their position and little could be done to change it. As Alan valued each and every guest at the hotel, it would definitely be a feather in her cap to keep the Delacortes from going elsewhere.

Sloane turned on her computer and pulled up the information they had on Russell and Penny Delacorte. They were from Las Vegas and had booked one of their most expensive suites for eight days. They had been there for three days with no reports of dissatisfaction, trouble with staff or other indications that might explain why they wanted out. The implication was that they would stay elsewhere, perhaps one of the other expensive resort hotels such as on Kaanapali Beach on Maui's western shore. Or maybe they were leaving the island altogether for some reason.

Sloane was primarily concerned with keeping them at the Island Shores, assuming they planned to stay on Maui for the next five days. She looked them up on the internet and discovered that Russell Delacorte was a fifty-six-year-old executive in the gambling industry. One year ago, he had married Penny Alvarez, a cocktail waitress who was thirty years his junior.

Sloane could only imagine what they were getting out of the relationship, but was happy if they were. She paid a visit to their suite. The door was opened by Russell Delacorte, whom she recognized from his photograph on the web.

"Aloha, Mr. Delacorte," she addressed him amiably. "I'm Sloane Hepburn, director of guest relations."

"Hi." He gazed at her steadily.

"Is your wife here?" Sloane asked.

"She's in the shower," he said.

Sloane's thin brows knitted. "I was hoping to talk to both of you."

"If this is about our decision to check out of the hotel—"

"Actually, it is," she confirmed. "Are you leaving the island or…"

"We're staying for five more days," he told her unapologetically.

"Can I ask why you want to leave the Island Shores?"

Russell ran a hand across his sagging chin, pausing as he looked in the direction of the bedroom. "It's my wife's doing. She's very high-maintenance and, well, just decided on a whim that she wanted to experience something else."

Sloane considered that perhaps if she spoke directly to his wife she might be able to get her to reconsider. "Is there anything I can do to maybe change her mind?"

"I don't think so," he said stiffly. "It's nothing personal. I think you have a great hotel and great food. But what Penny wants, Penny gets. Sorry."

Sloane gritted her teeth. It was obvious that she was fighting a losing battle here. Not that it was the end of the world. They had a right to sample more than one hotel on the island. She only hoped Alan agreed.

"Do you mind my asking which hotel you're moving to?" Sloane asked.

Russell shrugged. "Can't say. We're still working on that."

Sloane forced a smile. "If it doesn't work out, you're more than welcome to remain here."

"Thanks," he said.

"Have a good day."

Sloane walked away, feeling slightly irritated that her powers of persuasion had fallen short. That was life, though. All she could do was wish them well and turn her attention elsewhere. In this case that was Gene, always a most appealing distraction.

"I changed the sheets in the Beach Suite and we're all set for the next guests," Dayna told Gene as they met in the hallway.

"Excellent." He shook his head. "Sometimes I wonder what I'd ever do without you helping me out."

"I'm sure you'd do just fine." She giggled. "I appreciate your giving an old lady something to do other than play with the grandkids and knit."

"Believe me when I say it's been just as beneficial to me," Gene said. "When my ex left, it all seemed a bit overwhelming. Your presence has kept things very manageable for me."

"With a new lady in your life who I can see you adore, maybe someday she will fill those shoes in helping you to keep the bed-and-breakfast up and running smoothly."

Gene chuckled, having heard that before. "That's nice of you to say. Sloane's certainly a wonderful lady and would make a great host. However, she's already gainfully employed and, by all accounts, content in what she's doing."

Dayna's eyes crinkled. "Most women are truly only content when in love with the right man. Perhaps in you, Gene, she's found such a person. If so, and your feelings are the same for her, then anything else is possible."

Gene chewed on that thought after Dayna had left. There was no getting around the fact that Sloane made him feel things he hadn't felt in years, if ever. Maybe it was love that caused his heart to skip a beat whenever he thought of her. And made him feel restless when she wasn't around.

Were these sentiments the same for her? Could the

power of love carry their relationship in new directions both personally and professionally?

Gene's contemplation was broken when his cell phone rang. He got excited thinking that it was Sloane. Instead the caller was Neil Nagamine.

"Aloha," boomed Neil's voice.

"Hey," Gene muttered.

"How's business?"

"Pretty good."

"Hope it isn't too good for you, buddy," Neil said, "because I've just sent a couple your way."

"Oh, really?" Gene perked up.

"Yeah. They were in the office making arrangements for a cruise and spotted your brochure. The wife seemed hooked and I did my part to drum up support. They plan to give you a call. I wanted to give you a heads-up."

"As a matter of fact, a room just became available for the next week," Gene told him.

"I'm sure that will do the trick," Neil said. "A week's about what we come to expect from visitors."

"I'll be waiting for their call."

"Great. Hope they stay with you."

"So do I, and mahalo. I owe you one."

"You can pay me back by booking another cruise," Neil said. "Are you still seeing the sweet lady you brought aboard before?"

"Yeah, we're still together," Gene said happily.

"Figured as much. She may be a hard act for you to follow."

"I agree, she is." Gene wished he had met Sloane even sooner, while they were in a different place in their lives. No telling how far they might have come by now had circumstances brought them together on the mainland. "You'll definitely be hearing from me on another cruise."

He hung up, remembering how much fun and romance he and Sloane had created while cruising on the Pacific. Just as had been the case at the luau and in Hana. Seems like the magic between them went wherever they did, making him want to conjure it up that much more.

Gene went downstairs and was about to step aside when the phone rang. It was the couple Neil had referred. Gene gave them directions and then went to make sure everything in the Beach Suite was in order.

Chapter 12

"I just wanted to say hello," Sloane said, leaving the message on Gene's voice mail. She tossed out a few more words of affection. "Call me."

Sloane would have preferred hearing his deep voice talking back to her, but understood that Gene was working, just as she was. Tonight would be their time. They had already made plans to go out to dinner and make a night of it in his bed. She couldn't wait. The thought of making love to Gene well into the morning hours caused a reaction between Sloane's legs. It made her that much more excited at the prospect of how she would feel when Gene kissed her there, as he loved to do, and then put his hard penis inside her to induce an orgasm for both of them.

Cool down, she ordered herself, feeling moisture under her armpits. *Save it for later, when you can actually do something about it.*

Sloane made her rounds before spotting Alan near the

front desk. He was talking to another employee in what seemed to be a heated exchange. This suited her just fine, as she had hoped to avoid him for the time being after failing to keep the Delacortes as hotel guests. But just as Sloane was about to go in a different direction, Alan broke off abruptly from his conversation and headed her way.

She sucked in a deep breath. "Hello, Alan," she said, smiling to keep up appearances.

"Did you have any luck with the Delacortes?"

"Afraid not." Sloane wrinkled her nose. "It seems like they just want to try something else for a different flavor during their stay." She saw no reason to go into details about the high-maintenance, whimsical wife.

"Oh well, all you can do is try." Alan shrugged. "The room was already paid for and nonrefundable, so we didn't lose anything in the exchange."

Other than two guests who are staying somewhere else now. "You're right," Sloane said, and tried to soften the blow further. "Mr. Delacorte went out of his way to compliment the hotel and its service. I wouldn't be surprised if we got some repeat business from them during their next visit."

Alan clicked his expensive leather Oxfords together. "I'll believe it when I see it, but maybe that will happen."

Sloane smiled thinly and changed the subject to something else she needed to talk to him about while she had his attention.

"Welcome to Malloy's Bed and Breakfast," Gene said to the May-December couple identified as Russell and Penny Delacorte.

"We're happy to be here." Penny Russell spoke for them. She wiped a strand of blond hair from her brow. "When I saw your brochure, I fell in love with the place instantly and told Russell that we just *had* to stay here. Isn't that right, baby?"

"It sure is, honey," Russell said.

"That's nice." Gene grinned thoughtfully. He didn't bother to ask if they had stayed somewhere else before now and, if so, what had made them leave, as it wasn't any of his business. "I'll show you to your room and then give you the grand tour."

"Sounds good," Russell Delacorte said, and then kissed his wife passionately on the mouth.

The act of affection made Gene wish Sloane were there at that moment so he could kiss her soft, sensual lips. He suspended that thought for now, but planned to make up for it when Sloane came by this evening.

They stepped inside the Beach Suite, which faced the golden sand and offered a lovely view of the ocean. It had a king-size bed and a private lanai, and was the second-roomiest suite.

"It's terrific!" declared Penny, taking out her cell phone to get some pictures of it. "My mom will love this."

"I think you've got yourself a future guest," Russell told Gene. "Her mother loves to travel as much as we do."

That brought a smile to Gene's face. "She'll certainly be welcome here," he assured them.

After they had settled in, Gene introduced the couple to some of the other guests. He had also put out some tropical fruit and juices for everyone. As always, everyone seemed to get along well, and he did his part to encourage conversation and camaraderie. The Delacortes fit right in, indicating that while they usually stayed in luxury five-star resort hotels, the laid-back, friendly, quaint atmosphere of a bed-and-breakfast agreed with them.

Gene sensed that it was Russell's pretty young wife who called the shots. At least while they were there in Maui.

The older husband seemed perfectly willing to do whatever made Penny happy. Gene had no argument with that. He too wanted only to please the woman of his dreams.

It was clear to him that this woman was Sloane. She brought him to a whole new level of appreciation, intense desire and expectation, while he longed to be with her every moment of the day. If that wasn't love, then he didn't know what was.

I never thought I'd feel such affection for anyone again, Gene mused as he brought out some more snacks. But then he never imagined he'd meet someone like Sloane Hepburn on the beach that day, potentially changing his life forever.

The house was practically empty when Sloane arrived at Gene's B&B at seven. Apparently most of the guests were out and about doing their own thing. That was fine with her, as she had Gene all to herself. He was clearly just as happy, as he'd given her a kiss that left her head spinning.

"What was that for?" she asked him in his suite.

Gene gave her one of his thousand-watt grins. "Do I need a reason to kiss the best-looking woman in Maui?"

"Of course not." Sloane blushed, touching her tingling lips. "Kiss me as long and often as you like."

"Glad you see things my way."

He tilted her face and brought their lips together again for a mouth-heating kiss. Sloane got lost in the moment, pulling his lower lip into her mouth and sucking it salaciously. Her chest heaved and her breath quickened. Their lips locked passionately while their tongues searched for satisfaction, further tapping into Sloane's libido.

Before she knew it, they were in bed naked, making love. Gene took her from behind, allowing his penis to go deeper and at a more stimulating angle inside Sloane's vagina.

She clung to the pillow, digging her teeth into it while the sex went into overdrive. Her contractions were stronger and her satisfaction off the charts as Gene repeatedly hit the mark with his powerful thrusts and precise fingers simultaneously caressing her clitoris.

When her orgasm came, Sloane cried out joyously, unable to suppress her feelings of complete appeasement with Gene's erection still wedged deep inside her as he reached his own peak of sexual fulfillment.

Afterward, they held each other, the scent of their passion permeating Sloane's senses. She fell asleep with the vivid images of lovemaking in her head, along with feelings of love for Gene.

The following morning, Sloane joined Gene in preparing breakfast for his guests. On the long oak dining room table, she sat out a platter of fresh fruit, including sliced papayas and bananas, then brought in some bagels, yogurt, granola and tropical juices. Sloane used her skills in the kitchen and a little imagination to make French toast, adding ricotta cheese and macadamia nuts. Guests would have a choice of either guava or coconut syrup.

"We make a great team," Gene said, giving Sloane a kiss after sampling her French toast.

"You're just beginning to realize that?" She batted her eyes at him.

"Actually, I've known it for a while now. But I'm seeing it in more and more ways."

She used her pinkie to wipe cheese from the corner of his mouth. "Don't go getting any ideas. I'm not a cook per se, just helping out."

"And I appreciate it," he said evenly, wrapping his arms around her from behind. "It doesn't mean a man can't take advantage of his girlfriend's culinary abilities from time to time. Not to mention her sexual expertise in the bedroom."

Sloane giggled. "I wondered how long it would take you to get to that."

"Can you blame me?" Gene whispered into her ear.

"And just whose fault do you think it is that I'm so hot for you?"

"Mine," he said coolly. "Just as it's your fault I seem to have a one-track mind these days."

"So maybe we need to spend more time apart?" she teased.

"Or, better yet, less time apart so I get to see your lovely face and body even more!"

Sloane closed her eyes for a moment and fantasized about such a scenario. In an ideal world she would like nothing more than to be with Gene every second of the day. But since they lived apart, worked apart and weren't married, she didn't see that as being very realistic. Did he?

She wormed her way out of his arms. "We'll talk about that another time. We'd better finish up in the kitchen before your guests start coming in."

"Yeah, I suppose so," Gene muttered, and started a second pot of coffee.

"I'll get out the plates," Sloane said, grateful for the diversion when it was so difficult to get the man and his strong presence out of her mind.

Sloane walked into the dining room behind Gene and saw some guests seated. She homed in on the face of Russell Delacorte, who focused on her at the same time.

"Ms. Hepburn," he said.

"What are you doing here?" Sloane asked, though it was

obvious. She glanced at the young, attractive blonde who was cuddling up to him.

"I could ask you the same thing," Russell responded. "Looks like you're doing double duty…."

"Do you two know each other, Russ?" Penny Delacorte eyed Sloane sharply.

"I was about to ask the same thing," Gene said, a curious slant to his voice.

Sloane colored as she considered the awkward situation. "Mr. and Mrs. Delacorte were guests at the Island Shores before they checked out yesterday," she explained. "I didn't realize till now that they had checked into your bed-and-breakfast."

"So you're working for the competition too?" asked another guest amusingly. "This ought to be interesting."

"Actually, I'm the guest director at the Island Shores," Sloane said tersely. "Gene is my boyfriend." She met his eyes, wondering if he knew the Delacortes had stayed elsewhere prior to his accommodations.

"Small world," Gene said, grinning from one side of his mouth.

"We thought the Island Shores was great," Penny claimed. "We just needed to try something less intimidating and more down-to-earth. This bed-and-breakfast with its cozy, charming atmosphere right on the beach is perfect."

"Which is why Jill and I decided to stay here from the very beginning," said Lex Fromme of him and his wife. "It saved us the time, effort and cost of hotel hopping."

This got a laugh from some guests, while others seemed only mildly entertained and more interested in getting on with their day.

"Anyway, thank you for choosing Malloy's Bed and Breakfast," Gene told Russell and Penny, "even though it came at the expense of a fine hotel like the Island Shores."

"Their loss is your gain," Russell said bluntly while chewing a piece of French toast. "Thanks again, Ms. Hepburn, for your hospitality. I'm sure there are no hard feelings, all things considered." He winked at her.

Sloane forced a smile. "No hard feelings. You're entitled to stay wherever you wish on the island, and Malloy's Bed and Breakfast was certainly a nice choice."

"Then we're all in agreement." Russell lifted his fruit juice and the others followed suit.

Sloane took a deep breath and exhaled. Though she didn't blame this on Gene, and she knew the room had probably already been booked to someone looking for a last-minute deal at the Island Shores, it still irked Sloane for some reason that her place of employ had lost guests under her watch. She also doubted that Alan would be thrilled to know that they had taken their business to her boyfriend's bed-and-breakfast, as though there was a conflict of interest. Or was she making something out of nothing?

"So now you're stealing away our guests?" Sloane narrowed her eyes at Gene accusingly as they stood on the lanai.

His head snapped back as though she had slapped him. "You're joking, right?"

She paused. "You might have warned me that the Delacortes were staying here."

"I would have mentioned it if I had known they checked out of your hotel," Gene said.

"It was embarrassing to see them here this morning, after I had personally put in a plea to Russell Delacorte to stay at the hotel, but it fell on deaf ears. Apparently his wife was calling all the shots and he simply couldn't resist her youthful charm and sex appeal."

Gene couldn't resist a chuckle. "Can't say I blame him. If that's what floats his boat—pampering his young wife—why not give in to her prerogative?"

"That's not the point," Sloane snapped.

"Then what is?" Gene gave her a direct look. "What would you have had me do, turn away paying guests when I had a room available just because the Island Shores couldn't keep them content?"

"I never said that."

"Well, what are you saying?" he challenged her, hoping it wouldn't get him in hotter water.

"I'm not saying anything, okay?" She took a rueful breath. "Sorry for being a bitch. They're just two guests and, even if I was caught off guard, it's really no big deal."

"I'm happy we see eye to eye on that." Gene smiled, taking her hands. "No guests, wherever they came from, are more important to me than you."

"Even when I get on your case for something silly?" Sloane asked guiltily.

"Even if you do. It only builds character in a relationship. Besides—" he pulled her toward him "—you're sexy when you're a little pissed."

"Is that so?"

"Yeah. One eye gets a bit narrower than the other, and your lips curve down into a sexy pout." He traced his finger slowly across her lips. "And did I forget to mention that your caramel complexion darkens a couple of shades and wisps of smoke shoot out of your ears?"

"Enough!" Sloane laughed. "I get the picture."

"It would make a great picture to hang on my wall," Gene joked. "Or would it be better hanging on your wall?"

She squeezed his fingers. "You're really enjoying this, aren't you?"

"Way too much," he admitted. "But only because I am totally into you, no matter if you need an attitude adjustment from time to time or not."

She yanked her hands from his and playfully hit his shoulder. "I think it's you who needs the attitude adjustment, mister."

Gene chuckled. "I thought you wanted me just the way I am?"

"Maybe I do," she told him coquettishly.

"So show me how much you want me."

Sloane laughed. "What, you want me to rip your clothes off right here and now?"

The thought turned Gene on, but he didn't want to go quite that far right now. "I'll settle for a long, hot, juicy kiss."

"With an emphasis on *juicy,*" she sang with amusement.

"Just kiss me—let me taste those pouty lips and I'll be in heaven."

Sloane moved closer. "All right, I'll be your angel and give you a slice of heaven in Maui."

She held his cheeks and kissed Gene on the mouth, slipping her tongue between his teeth. He sucked her soft lips as though they provided nourishment.

When they finally broke away from each other, Sloane looked at him with eyes full of emotion. He'd never seen her look more beautiful.

"That was some kiss," he told her, licking his lips. "You're definitely an angel."

"I'm also a lady who loves you," she cooed, her eyes locked with his.

"What?" Gene wanted to make sure he understood her meaning as his heart skipped a beat.

"I've fallen in love with you, Gene Malloy. I sure hope you can handle it."

Chapter 13

There, I said it. Now what happens? Sloane wondered if she had been premature in sharing her thoughts. She could not read the expression on Gene's face to know what his response would be, making her sweat it out till he said something. Her greatest hope was that the feeling was mutual.

"I can handle learning your feelings," he said levelly, his brown-gray eyes peering at Sloane. "It's something I've wanted to hear you say."

"And what about you?" Sloane gazed at him with nervous anticipation.

Gene kept a straight face. "I think I've known for some time now that I love you. I was just waiting for the right time to say it."

Right time? Her heart fluttered with delight. "Are you sure you wouldn't have kept this little secret to yourself forever had I not spoken up?"

He chuckled cutely. "Not a chance. You're far too important to me to have remained mute and risked allowing my window of opportunity to pass us both by. I'm not afraid to say I love you, Sloane, or to accept your love for me."

His words warmed her. "I'd have to say the same thing."

Gene angled his head and kissed her, making sure she felt it from her head to her toes before stepping back. "You might say that was sealing the deal."

Sloane touched her tingling lips. It only confirmed what was already abundantly clear: Gene had an effect on her like no other, producing sexual feelings that had grown into love.

Her eyes lifted to meet his. "So now that we have sealed our love, where do we go from here?" *I don't want to set my expectations too high.*

"How about to the beach?" Gene responded succinctly.

"The beach?"

He smiled. "Yeah. It's a nice day. Let's take a walk."

That wasn't quite what Sloane was expecting in response to her question. But since she had the day off and there was nothing she wanted to do more than spend time with the man she'd just admitted loving, a beach walk could be romantic.

"All right, we'll walk," she told him.

A few minutes later, they left the bed-and-breakfast and walked down the path leading to the beach. Gene took Sloane's hand as they moved barefoot through the soft sand.

"After my divorce, I wasn't sure if I'd ever find love again," he admitted.

"I wasn't exactly expecting to fall in love either when I moved to Maui," Sloane said.

"Guess we were both in for a surprise."

She regarded his profile. "Does it scare you?"

He gave her a steady look. "No. Quite the contrary, it's renewed my faith in human nature and my ability to rediscover what's been in me all along."

"You mean love?" she asked.

"Yeah, and being open enough to allow it to spring to life when the right person came along."

"I thought falling in love would only hinder my work ethic," Sloane admitted, "leaving me reluctant to go down that path. But I was wrong. Meeting you and having a romance like never before has opened my eyes in ways I never thought possible."

Gene grinned. "Putting our love cards on the table will make things even better for us," he declared. "Now every time we make love, it won't only be about the wonderful sex between us, but the emotional connection that drives it."

"True." Sloane felt a stirring within as she pondered the new level their relationship was entering. "I guess this means we're in a committed romance."

"It sure does," Gene affirmed. "In reality, that's been the case from the moment we started seeing each other, as I haven't had my eye on anyone else."

"Me neither," Sloane said. "You're the only one I've been interested in since I came to Maui, and I'm very content with that."

Gene stopped and faced her. "So am I—content that I happen to be involved with the loveliest lady in Hawaii or anywhere else. I say let's enjoy the journey we've embarked on and make the most of wherever it leads us."

"I want that, too." Sloane held his gaze before resting her eyes on Gene's generous mouth. She needed him to kiss her in that moment.

He answered her silent plea, positioning his face and moving his lips onto hers. Sloane embraced the kiss as she did the man himself, with passion and promise. She wanted only to love Gene and test the limits of that love for all it was worth.

That afternoon, Gene went into town for supplies. His mind was still on Sloane, who had gone home. He expected her back later for another round in bed and possibly further discussion about their feelings. Gene hadn't anticipated that Sloane's minor annoyance with the Delacortes' stay at his bed-and-breakfast would lead to him and Sloane professing their love for each other. Yet it had only been a matter of time before they declared their feelings to each other.

For his part, Gene had known early on that Sloane was someone very special with whom he could possibly fall in love. She had managed to steal his heart and give him a whole new and exciting reason for living. And to know that her feelings for him were just as strong floored Gene. What more could he have asked for than coming to the aid of a gorgeous, sexier-than-she-imagined woman and falling for her, while getting the same in return?

Rather than simply accepting his good fortune, Gene wanted to make sure it never went away. But how could he be certain of that? He'd already gone through the marriage thing and learned the hard way that it offered no guarantees and, in his case, only heartbreak and disappointment.

Could it be different with Sloane? Or was that a direction she still had little interest in, with her professional objectives taking priority?

What Gene didn't want was to mess things up by applying undue pressure or making demands that might backfire, driving Sloane away. Not to mention he wasn't sure what the hell he wanted beyond the love and lust they gave each other. Maybe that was enough in and of itself to sustain them. Or maybe the more they gave of themselves, the more they would want or demand.

For now, Gene intended to immerse himself in the new direction their relationship had taken that made him feel higher than the clouds and had him thinking ahead to tomorrow and the day after.

Sloane welcomed the group from New Orleans to the Island Shores. They were assembled in a conference room where she would tell them about various activities they had arranged that were designed to keep them engaged while their spouses were at business meetings. She wasn't too sure they all were on the same page, which was why her choices had a range of appeal.

"Aloha, everyone," she said, getting their attention. "We are so pleased that you've come to Maui with your spouses to enjoy some fun and frolic away from home. I've put together an amazing itinerary that I'm sure everyone will enjoy. But first, let me tell you a bit about Maui and what makes it the best of the Hawaiian Islands."

After doing her best to promote Maui, Sloane was ready to offer her program for keeping them busy while satisfying the overall objectives of the corporate gathering at the Island Shores.

"For today, I thought we'd start off with a visit to the Maui Arts and Cultural Center," Sloane stated. "It's located on the north shore of central Maui in Kahului, not far from the airport. After lunch, our next stop will be Lahaina, which means 'merciless sun' for its hot weather at this time of year. Lahaina is located in West Maui and known for its famous Front Street with fine art galleries and numerous interesting shops."

Sloane outlined the other activities she'd planned for

the next few days, including hanging out on Kaanapali Beach, snorkeling in Kapalua Bay, visiting the Bailey House Museum in Wailuku and Maui Mall, going on a supper cruise and, on their last day, enjoying a luau at the Island Shores Resort.

Whew, that went about as well as could be expected, Sloane told herself after it was over. She was pleased that she had put together a well-rounded itinerary for the group. Now the hard part was making sure everything went without a hitch.

A couple of hours later, Sloane was still on her feet and feeling sorely in need of a foot massage. She knew Gene would be happy to be her masseur, as he had expertly soothed her tired feet several other times, giving special attention to each toe and her heels. Then afterward he would be more than welcome to rub down and stroke other parts of her body.

Sloane's phone rang, jarring her from those sensual thoughts. It was her girlfriend, Gail.

"Hey there," Sloane said pleasantly.

"I need to get away from here," Gail complained.

"What happened?"

"What didn't happen is a better question," Gail snorted. "Went on a blind date that was a total disaster. Business is good, but I had a falling-out with a supplier. Oh, and did I mention that my mother was here for a week getting on my case about being single, too thin and needing a makeover? Need I say more?"

Sloane suppressed a chuckle, though she felt bad for her. "Sounds like you have had it rough."

"I'd like to come to Maui for a few days, clear my head and have some fun for a change."

Sloane quickly adjusted to the surprise news. "That sounds fine. When?"

"This Friday through Sunday," Gail said. "I know it's short notice, but—"

"Don't be silly," Sloane broke in. "You're more than welcome to stay with me."

"Who said anything about staying with you? I'm sure your sofa is comfortable and your bed, too, but I'd rather not put you out." Gail sighed. "I'd like to stay at your man's bed-and-breakfast, if there's a room available."

"Hmm." Sloane knew that Gene's suites were often booked months in advance. "I'll give him a call to see if he has anything."

"Thanks," Gail's said. "I want to check out this Gene Malloy myself in his own environment to see if he really passes muster in romancing my best friend."

A chuckle escaped Sloane's throat. She could imagine Gail giving Gene the third degree and him looking at her as if she were crazy. On the other hand, if Gene really was to become a fixture in her life, she wanted him and Gail to get along, just as Gene wanted her to like Walter and Talia, and vice versa.

"You'll see for yourself what a terrific guy he is," Sloane told her confidently. "I'm sure he'll like you, too—but not too much."

Gail chuckled. "Don't worry, I'll keep my hands to myself."

"You'd better." Sloane laughed. "Actually, I think it would be great if you stayed at his bed-and-breakfast. That way you could interact with the other guests and not find yourself bored to death while I'm at work."

"Fat chance of that," Gail said. "If I'm going to fly across the country and ocean, you can be damn sure that I won't allow myself to be bored in Hawaii."

"Good point," Sloane said. "And who knows, you might even find Mr. Right in Maui, just like I did."

"That would be nice," Gail said dreamily. "I could sell my business and reopen it there, or follow my dream man wherever he happened to be from."

"Before we get too ahead of ourselves, let's make sure Gene has a room," Sloane told her. "Or, if that fails, I can get you a nice room at the Island Shores."

"Sounds like a plan," Gail said. "I'll wait to hear from you."

Sloane disconnected and called Gene. He picked up right away.

"Hello, beautiful," he said sweetly.

She beamed at hearing his appealing voice and flattery. "Do you happen to have a suite open this weekend?" *Say yes, please.*

"As a matter of fact, I do. The couple in the Paradise Suite is checking out on Thursday and the room will be free for the next week."

"Perfect," Sloane said. "My girlfriend, Gail, from Raleigh, wants to fly in for a few days. I could put her at the Island Shores, but I wanted to try you first."

"That was thoughtful," Gene said. "I'd be delighted to play host for your friend."

Sloane smiled. "Great! I'll tell her."

"I'm sure she'll be checking me out, so I guess I should be on my best behavior," he joked.

"Aren't you always?"

"For the most part." Gene chuckled. "I admit to being a bit naughty when I'm in bed with you."

"Just a bit naughty?" Sloane asked.

"Okay, a lot," Gene said, chuckling lasciviously.

"That's more like it."

"I haven't heard any complaints from you."

"That's because there are none," she conceded, blushing. "You do your thing exceedingly well in the bedroom."

"I'll do whatever it takes to put a smile on your face when the deed is done," Gene promised.

"You just keep doing your deeds and I'll keep smiling," Sloane murmured, feeling hot all over.

Gene laughed. "It's a deal."

She lifted one heel of her pump off the floor, relieving the soreness. "I think what I could use most right now is a foot massage. Think you could help me out there?"

"It would be my pleasure to give your feet a nice massage. Shall I come to your place or do you want to come to mine?"

"You can come over," she told him. "I should be home in about an hour."

"I'll see you then," he said. "I promise your feet will get extra-special attention, along with any other body parts that need tending to."

"I'm counting on it." Sloane smiled. "Bye for now. Love you."

"Love you, too," Gene responded.

Sloane loved hearing those words of endearment from Gene, just as she felt good being able to say the same to him. Things were certainly looking up for her these days. Was that a sign that the future would be even brighter?

Sloane picked up Gail at the airport, excited that her friend would be there to share a bit of quality time. *I probably should have invited her sooner, but there was just too much going on.* Including a magical romance with Gene, who had stolen her heart and filled her with joy. Maybe Gail would be as fortunate after being with one too many losers.

Sloane spotted Gail as she emerged into the sunlight. Both broke into a smile.

"Hey, girl," Gail said.

"Aloha," Sloane replied, keeping up with her now-routine Hawaiian greeting. She put a flower lei around her neck.

"Aloha." Gail set her bag down and the two embraced. She stepped back and studied Sloane. "Well, look at you."

Sloane blushed. She wore a light yellow V-neck tee, navy blue walking shorts, and sandals. Her hair was pulled back into a ponytail and she wore almost no makeup on her flawless caramel skin.

"Look at you," Sloane turned the tables on her friend. She and Gail were around the same height and build. Gail had curly short brunette hair and small brown eyes. "You've still got it going on, I see."

"We both do." Gail grinned. "I can't believe I'm really in Maui."

"Well, believe it!" Sloane laughed. "I had the same reaction when I first got here."

Gail's lashes fluttered. "And look how far you've come with Mr. Malloy since that time."

A self-conscious smile crossed Sloane's face. "Yes, I guess you could say there's been some progress in our relationship. But more on that later. Let's get going so you can check in."

"Sounds good. I'm really looking forward to this mini vacation to get away from it all," Gail said.

Sloane smiled. "Yes, it will do you a world of good."

A few minutes later, they were on Mokulele Highway en route to Wailea.

"You weren't exaggerating when you said how beautiful it is here," remarked Gail as she looked out the window.

"I could never put into words just how breathtaking Maui is," Sloane told her.

"Does it ever freak you out, being separated from the mainland by all this water?" Gail asked curiously.

Sloane thought about it. "Not really. While Maui is definitely miles apart from Raleigh, literally and figuratively, you get used to it after a while and don't even think about it being an island. Except when it comes to promoting Maui as part of my job."

Gail turned to her. "Speaking of which, now that your job is no longer a top priority, are you still getting as much out of it?"

Sloane glanced away from the steering wheel. "Of course," she said. "I love my job. I can still be a hotel guest director and have a boyfriend."

"I realize that. But since moving here was all about a great career opportunity, finding romance with an incredible guy has to have some effect on your getting up and going to work every day."

"All right, at times, it is harder to be apart from Gene when duty calls," Sloane confessed. "He's tapped into a side of me I didn't even know existed. And so, yes, I sometimes lose my focus at work while thinking about him and wanting to be with him. But I just contain those thoughts and try to keep my eye on the ball."

"I can barely wait to meet the man who put a hex on you," Gail said. "Or is it the other way around?"

"I think we've both gotten caught under each other's spell." Sloane smiled. "At least it seems like he's every bit as much into me as I am into him."

"Does that mean you see wedding bells in your future?"

Sloane sighed. "We haven't talked about that." Not since they had declared their love for each other. Was Gene still opposed to marriage? Or were they both holding back from throwing the notion out there?

"But I assume you're not as opposed to it as before?" Gail asked.

"I suppose I'm not," Sloane had to admit. "That doesn't mean we're moving in that direction. We're still coming to terms with being in love."

"I really envy you, especially since my love life sucks."

"It's only a temporary bump in the road," suggested Sloane.

Gail raised a brow. "You really think so?"

"Yes. I'm sure there's someone out there for you. You just need to be patient."

"Easy for you to say, when you've got a man willing to wait on you for everything," Gail moaned. "I just seem to keep going around in circles."

Sloane gave her a placating smile. "First of all, Gene is not my servant, though he is very attentive in and out of bed. Second, you can break the circle game by not trying so hard and maybe opening your mind to new possibilities."

"You mean like finding a man in Maui?" Gail asked.

"Sure, why not?" Sloane looked at her. "Or California. Or New York. Or the Bahamas. My point is there are a lot of good men out there. You just may have to be more creative to find them."

"Or be in the right place at the right time like you were," Gail suggested.

"That too," Sloane said, offering her a friendly grin.

Gail sighed. "So is there anything I need to know about Gene before we get there?"

"Such as?"

"Oh, I don't know. Is he full of himself, hot-tempered, condescending, superficial, things like that?"

Sloane laughed. "None of the above. Gene is one of the good guys and he's seriously into me. He'll make you feel right at home like he does all his guests."

"Sounds like the perfect host."

"I think he is," Sloane said. The perfect man to have in her life and someone she wanted to build her world around, piece by piece.

Chapter 14

Gene was standing on the lanai when Sloane's car pulled into the driveway. He could see Gail on the passenger side. He was a little nervous meeting Sloane's best friend. He knew first impressions meant just that—you didn't get a second chance. As such, he wanted to make it count, knowing that Gail would undoubtedly be checking him out, looking to give Sloane the thumbs-up or thumbs-down as to whether or not he made the grade in her book. He didn't intend to make it easy for Gail to diminish the enthusiasm he and Sloane shared for their relationship and burgeoning love.

He stepped down to greet them as they got out of the car. "I see my latest guest has arrived."

"Safe and sound," Sloane said.

Gene gave her a quick peck on the lips, and then turned his attention to her friend. "You must be Gail?"

"That's me." She gazed at him with a big grin on her face. "And you must be Gene?"

"Right again," he said, wondering what Sloane had told her about him, considering he knew little about her.

"Well, it looks like no introductions will be necessary," Sloane said humorously.

Gene shook Gail's small hand, engulfing it in his. "Nice to meet you."

"Same here," Gail said.

"Welcome to Maui and Malloy's Bed and Breakfast," he told her.

"Thank you." Gail looked around at the scenery. "I'm excited to be here."

"Let's get you settled into your suite and then Sloane and I can show you around."

"I'd like that," she said.

Gene grabbed her bag with one hand and used the other to hold Sloane's hand. He winked at her and she smiled at him. Knowing how gratifying it had been to have his friends visit recently, he was happy she would have the same experience.

An hour later, Gene had prepared some cinnamon toast and cheddar cheese omelets. He also set out bagels and a fresh-fruit platter along with assorted beverages for Gail and his other guests. It was well beyond breakfast hours, but he made an exception in this case, knowing Gail was hungry and wanting to appease that without going to a local restaurant.

"She seems to be fitting right in," he told Sloane when they had a moment alone.

"Did you think she wouldn't?" Sloane questioned.

Gene grinned. "Just the opposite. I was sure that the warm, friendly atmosphere I've created would make Gail feel totally at ease and allow her to be a part of this wonderful experience of paradise and camaraderie."

"Well, you were right. She loves being here and chatting with the other guests. I may have trouble dragging her away for some girlfriend time."

Gene chuckled, taking her into his arms. "Would that be so bad? It would just leave more time for you to spend with your boyfriend." He kissed her, his lips lingering on her open mouth for a moment or two.

Sloane pulled her mouth away and ran her tongue across her lips. "Believe me, that's nice, but since Gail will be here for less than three days, I really want to make the most of our time. Hope you can understand that?"

"Of course," he assured her, pulling back his desire to have her all to himself. "Spend all the time you want with Gail, catching up and everything. But since she's staying here rather than at your place, I assume she also wants to see what life is like in Maui."

"She does," Sloane said. "Especially while I'm at work. I couldn't really get the time off on such short notice."

"I'll take good care of your friend in your absence." Gene eyed her.

"Just don't take care of her too much," Sloane warned.

Gene laughed. "A little jealous, are we?"

"Not at all," she said. "I'm just playing with you. I'm sure you'll take good care of Gail while I'm working."

"Guaranteed."

"I have to warn you, though. Be prepared for a grilling."

"Oh…?" Gene's gaze lowered to her eyes.

Sloane paused. "Knowing Gail, I'm sure she will try to see what you're made of and if you're really good boyfriend material for me."

"I see." Gene scratched his jaw thoughtfully. "Thanks

for the warning. I'll brace myself for anything she throws at me. As for good boyfriend material, that's really for you to determine. But I understand that friends have to add their two cents."

"I thought you would," Sloane said, smiling. "Regarding boyfriend material, you're doing just fine in my book, so far."

"And I plan to keep it that way." He put his arm around her and pulled her toward him for another kiss, forcing himself to end it. "Let's find Gail and see what she's up to."

That night, Sloane and Gene took Gail to a nightclub in nearby Kihei. They managed to find a table, even though the place was packed with a combination of tourists and locals. Sloane and Gail ordered pina coladas, and Gene ordered a Blue Hawaiian.

"Having fun?" Sloane asked her friend after an hour of drinks and good music.

"Yes, it sure beats sitting home alone like I was doing a week ago," Gail said.

"Forget about that." Sloane patted her hand. "You're here now."

"True." Gail sipped her drink. "And so are you two. Must be karma or something the way you met."

Sloane faced Gene. "I don't know about that. What do you think?"

He flashed a stunning smile at her. "Hey, I'm all about destiny. What are the chances I would have met you on the mainland?"

"Probably one in a million," she conceded.

"More like one in a trillion," he suggested. "I like the odds much better here on the island of Maui."

"Wonder if lightning could strike twice?" joked Gail.

"Only if you don't mind getting drenched by a wave," Gene said wryly.

She laughed. "Oh, so that's a prerequisite for meeting my knight in shining armor—being sucker punched by a wave?"

"I wouldn't go that far," Sloane jumped in. "You're gorgeous, smart, successful and single. I'd say that's enough to meet a man under any circumstances."

"You think so?" Gail rolled her eyes skeptically. "Seems like that's what causes the good ones to run the other way, present company excluded."

Gene grinned. "Guess I'm the exception to the rule. I'd never run away from the likes of Sloane, who just described herself to a tee."

"Other than being single," Gail noted.

"Right. She's definitely attached these days."

"That's for sure," Sloane said, looking at him starry-eyed. "Having you in my life has taken away any thoughts of being happily single."

"Same here," Gene assured her.

She leaned over and kissed him. The kiss might have gone on forever, but Sloane stopped it, wanting the outing to be more about Gail enjoying the nightlife in Maui than having her feel like she was the third wheel.

Sloane intended to pick up where the kiss left off tonight when they were in bed. She'd picked out a sexy teddy that she hoped would seduce Gene. It would be up to him whether or not she kept it on all night.

The next day, Gene was up early as usual, setting out breakfast for his guests. He hadn't gotten much sleep, as Sloane wouldn't allow it. Instead they made love for much of the night, enjoying the contours of each other's bodies.

She had headed back to her condo to freshen up before going to work.

This meant he would have to spend some time with Gail without Sloane's presence. Gene welcomed the challenge of the "grilling" Sloane suggested Gail had in store for him. It would also give him the opportunity to have some one-on-one time of his own to see what other tidbits he could learn about Sloane from someone who knew her before he did.

Gene had watched guests come and go this morning, and assumed Gail was still getting her beauty rest to make up for last night and maybe a few too many cocktails. He was thinking about knocking on her door to wake her up to some hot coffee and food when Gene saw her walk in the front door.

"You're up," he said, surprised.

"Of course." Gail offered a smile. "Did you think I'd waste my precious time here by sleeping?"

Gene chuckled unevenly. "I thought maybe you'd need to sleep it off."

"No more than you," she tossed at him. "I seem to recall you matched me drink for drink."

He didn't quite remember it that way, but left it alone. "Good point. Can I make you a cup of coffee or tea?"

"Coffee's good, no sugar. Let me just go wash my face and I'll be right with you."

Gene made two cups of coffee and brought them to the living room. He brought the tray of yogurt, blueberries, macadamia nuts and English muffins from the lanai and put it on the coffee table, along with dishware. He grabbed a few of the macadamia nuts and tossed them in his mouth while looking around the place he had turned into a successful business. Sometimes it still seemed unbelievable that the place was his. The fact that he was going it alone continued to rub him the wrong way, even if once it seemed as if that was the way it was meant to be.

The more he thought about it, the more Gene wished Sloane were operating this bed-and-breakfast with him. She had the right type of personality to be a great hostess and add a woman's touch that was missing, no disrespect to Dayna. Not to mention as his romantic mate, Sloane's regular presence would be felt in the bedroom and throughout the house. Would she ever consider such a proposition? Or would it be foolish to even ask?

"Where is everybody?" Gail asked, snapping him from his thoughts.

Gene looked at her and grinned. "Like you, they're usually up and at it early, not wanting to waste a moment hanging around the accommodations."

"Does that bother you?"

"Not at all," he assured her. "I'm very proud of my bed-and-breakfast, and most guests leave with a favorable opinion. But this isn't why they come to Maui. Far from it. With so many interesting things to see and do, I wouldn't expect anyone to miss out by keeping me company."

Gail chuckled. "Nice way of putting it."

"There's your coffee," Gene pointed out. "And breakfast. Help yourself."

"I will, thanks." She put a few items on a plate and sat down, pausing. "I don't think I've ever seen Sloane as happy in a relationship. In fact, I'm not sure she's ever had a true involvement with a man before now."

"I gathered as much," Gene said. "I guess she was just waiting for someone to show up who could appeal to her on the same level she appealed to him."

"Someone like you?"

"Yeah. We seem to have hit all the right notes in making this work."

Gail peered at him beneath her coffee mug. "So what exactly are your intentions concerning Sloane?"

Gene cocked a brow, though he'd suspected she might come at him from that direction. "My intentions are to keep our relationship going and do my part not to mess this up."

"Did you mess up things in your marriage?" she asked bluntly.

He stiffened. "I won't go so far as to say I was faultless in my marriage breakdown," he said. "We both made mistakes. I've certainly learned from mine."

"Enough that you could see yourself marrying again?" Gail wondered.

"Yeah, I can see that. Maybe not today, but down the line."

"Whatever happens between you and Sloane, I hope you'll always be honest with her. She deserves that."

"I agree," Gene said, raising his mug. "I'll never hurt her intentionally."

"Men always say that, as if unintentionally hurts less," Gail uttered sarcastically. "All I'm saying is that I want my best friend to be happy with someone who will always have her best interests at heart."

"You're singing to the band," he said tonelessly. "You and I are on the same page. I think Sloane is sharp enough to figure out what—and who—makes her happy, don't you?"

"I suppose." Gail scooped some yogurt with a spoon. "I'm not trying to meddle. Just being a good friend."

"I know. I respect that." Gene had gotten no less from Walter and Talia, who had given their clear approval of Sloane. This seemed like an ideal time to ask a few questions himself. "Has Sloane always been driven to succeed on a professional level?"

"I'd say yes, for as long as I've known her," Gail answered. "I think it may have something to do with needing to prove herself and being in control of the situation."

Gene cast his eyes at her thoughtfully. "As opposed to matters of the heart?"

She smiled faintly. "Something like that."

"Do you think she could ever walk away from her job?"

Gail's eyes widened. "For what?"

Gene decided it was best not to suggest anything that might get back to Sloane prematurely. "Oh, nothing in particular. I'm just curious to see if you think the job will always be the center of her universe."

"Actually, I think you're the center of her universe at the moment," Gail told him. "Yes, her job will always be important. But there are other things even more important, and I think she's starting to realize that."

So am I. And Sloane Hepburn is at the top of the list. Gene sat on that thought as he finished his coffee.

That afternoon, Sloane introduced Gail to some of the staff at the Island Shores and then gave her a tour, hoping she wouldn't get so caught up in its grandness that she might have second thoughts about staying at Gene's bed-and-breakfast. But her friend seemed to take it all in stride, as though having seen one resort hotel she had seen them all.

This was fine by Sloane, as the one thing she didn't want was to compete with Gene when it came to business. She loved being at his bed-and-breakfast and felt that it offered just as much in many respects as any five-star hotel. Only it cost less and offered more personal attention from an incredible host.

She treated Gail to lunch in the hotel, sensing her friend

was eager to give her report card on Gene now that they had spent time together. Admittedly, Sloane was just as eager to hear her thoughts.

"Well, I'm sure you're wondering if I talked to Gene…" Gail smiled at Sloane while moving her stir-fried chicken around the plate.

"The thought crossed my mind," Sloane admitted, forking vegetables swimming in cream sauce. "I figured you'd get around to telling me, if there was anything worth saying."

Gail paused deliberately. "The man's really into you," she stated emphatically.

"Is he now?" Sloane batted her lashes as though this was a surprise to her. "Tell me more…"

"As your friend, I didn't pull any punches in asking Gene about his feelings toward you, where he saw this going, and even his failed marriage."

This ought to be interesting. "And…?"

"Gene didn't flinch. He responded straightforwardly, wearing his heart on his sleeve." Gail met Sloane's eyes. "I came away feeling that he wants this to work for the long term and is committed to doing his part to make that happen."

Sloane had already believed that was the case, but was happy Gene had opened up to Gail, just as Sloane had to Talia. *We've both reached the point where there's no holding back in what we want out of this relationship.*

"Thanks for having my back," Sloane told Gail, "but it wasn't necessary. Gene's been good to me and for me, otherwise I never would have fallen in love with him."

"Do you love him more than your job?"

Sloane's eyes widened. "What?"

"You heard me," Gail stated tersely.

"Why are you asking me that?"

Gail regarded her. "It's an honest question and deserves an honest answer."

Sloane wrinkled her nose. "Where is this coming from?" Had Gene put her up to it?

"I'm not trying to stir up trouble," Gail insisted. "I just want to make sure you have your priorities in order. A good man is always more important than a good job."

"I realize that," Sloane said defensively, even though she had always been driven by the job without having a man in her life. "But why can't one have both?"

"You can—and do, in fact. Just be true to your feelings and allow them to blossom in carrying you as far as they're meant to."

"I intend to do just that," Sloane promised.

"Yeah?"

"Yes, yes." Sloane laughed. "You don't have to worry about me. I'll be fine. So will Gene. We're happy together."

"I can see that." Gail forked a boneless chicken cube. "You go, girl." She raised her hand and gave Sloane a high five. "And I'll be back whenever you get around to saying 'I do' with Gene."

Sloane's mouth became a perfect O. "Did I say anything about getting married?" Had Gene?

"No. I'm just putting that out there."

"Well, put it back in there," Sloane said, slicing into her fish. "I love Gene, but I'm not sure if being his second wife is in the cards."

"Why not?" Gail looked at her sharply. "And please don't say because you and marriage don't mix."

"We do mix." Sloane sighed. "For the longest time I wasn't sure about that. Now I am."

"Then, what?"

"I have to be sure Gene feels the same way."

"He loves you," Gail argued.

"I know," Sloane told her. "We'll have to see if he loves me enough to ask for my hand in marriage without my prompting him to do so. Or being scared off by the been-there, done-that thing."

Until such a time, she wouldn't get her hopes up that a ring was forthcoming. Gene was everything she wanted in a man and she would love being his wife. But he had to want that too. Then they could have the type of life that Sloane had never thought possible for herself till now. Only the man who had captured her heart could make that happen.

Chapter 15

On Sunday evening, Gene drove over to Sloane's place with a bottle of Ulupalakua red wine. Earlier in the day, he had accompanied her and Gail to the Whaler's Village Museum and Lahaina Banyan Tree Park, before Sloane drove her friend to the airport. Gene liked Gail and was sure he'd see her again one day, especially since he fully intended for Sloane to be a big part of his life for years to come.

Right now his only thoughts were on Sloane and building upon their commitment to each other. In his mind, that meant spending more time together and combining their talents in a way that would bring out the best in one another while the love they shared continued to grow by leaps and bounds. Gene wasn't sure how Sloane would react to his suggestion and, frankly, was a bit nervous at the prospect. But he'd thought this over long and hard and would see it through, knowing that it wouldn't affect their relationship one way or the other as far as he was concerned.

When Sloane opened the door, Gene found it impossible not to be turned on as she stood there in body-hugging loungewear.

"Hey," he said, grinning.

"Hi, handsome." She flashed him an enticing smile.

He kissed her, savoring her taste for a moment of pleasure. "I brought some wine."

"Wonderful." Sloane beamed, taking the bottle. "Another great selection."

"I know my wine," Gene said.

"Let's go break it in."

Gene followed her into the kitchen and watched as she took out a couple of goblets. He came up behind her, put his arms around her waist, and kissed her hair. "I've missed you."

"I haven't gone anywhere," she said over her shoulder.

"You've been preoccupied."

Sloane's eyes twinkled. "Don't want to share me with anyone, huh?"

"Not if I can help it," he replied.

"Gail's gone now."

He turned her to face him. "I can see that."

"So you have me all to yourself again."

Gene's dimples deepened seductively. "I like that." He kissed her, sucking her lower lip. "I like it a lot."

Sloane broke away from his mouth, her lashes fluttering. "What about all those guests I have to share you with?"

"They will never have any part of me that I've given to you," he promised.

"That's good to know," she said with a smile.

Gene poured wine into the glasses and held one up to Sloane's mouth. Once she'd taken a sip, he set the glass down and gave her a passionate kiss, tasting the wine on her wet lips. He felt himself becoming aroused, practically wanting to take her right there on the spot.

Instead, he would take her to bed. What he had to say could wait until a little later. Getting between her legs couldn't.

Sloane straddled Gene's hard body and galloped atop him lustfully as his erection impaled her, going deeper and deeper as she went farther down on him. Her hands clutched the sheet and her eyes squeezed shut while his fingers gently rubbed her nipples. They were both slick with perspiration from the lengthy lovemaking and frequent changes of position. Sloane made her vagina constrict around Gene's penis, knowing this spurred him on even more, which in turn enhanced the experience for her.

After moving steadily up and down the span of him to the sounds of Gene's guttural groans, Sloane's body craved satisfaction. She leaned down onto his chest, bringing their bodies close together for the final ascent of orgasmic bliss.

"I'm coming," she cried out as her body began to quiver violently.

"Go right ahead, baby," Gene moaned. "I'm with you all the way."

He grabbed a firm hold of Sloane's buttocks and squeezed them while bringing her down hard upon his erection and keeping her there so she could feel him throbbing against her very core. She sought out his mouth, kissing him passionately with her lips, tongue and teeth, needing to feel the power and taste of his kisses. Gene complied as he conquered her lips with his, panting as they breathed into each other's mouths.

They rocked the bed and immersed themselves in the torrid sex that locked their bodies as one, holding nothing back when the moment of impact erupted all at once, bringing them to heated fruition and then a slow return to normal breathing.

Sloane licked Gene's lips a final joyous time before slumping onto the bed, wanting only to be held by her man while they absorbed the remnants of their passion. She had nearly fallen asleep, content that no words were necessary to speak of their incredibly satisfying actions, when Gene tapped on her shoulder.

"You itching for another round?" Sloane whispered. The idea didn't surprise her one bit, as it seemed he could never get enough of her.

"Actually, I want to talk to you…." he said in a low voice.

She raised her face. "Sounds serious. Or is that your after-sex voice?"

He maintained a straight look. "I want you to move in with me."

"What?" Sloane met his eyes.

"I'd like us to run the bed-and-breakfast together," Gene said. "I know we could do a hell of a job as a team to keep the place running successfully."

Sloane was almost speechless. She replayed his words in her head, shocked as much by what he said as what he didn't say. She heard nothing about wanting her to live with him for love, much less a proposal of marriage.

"That sounds interesting, but I already have a job," she responded, as though this had somehow escaped him.

"I understand that." He paused, a firm leg draped across hers. "But that's all it is, a job. What I'm asking you for is the opportunity to build something together as part of our growing relationship—"

"Wait a minute," Sloane interrupted him, ignoring the sensation of their skin touching. "Are you saying that our relationship should be tied to operating your bed-and-breakfast?"

Gene chuckled humorlessly. "Of course not. The two are totally different entities. I'm only saying they could be tied together if we wanted that by using our professional skills to make the bed-and-breakfast the best it can be. That has nothing to do with the love I feel for you."

"Excuse me, but it sounds like it has everything to do with that," she had to say. "You can't just lay on me out of the blue that you want me to break my lease, quit my job, and come work for you."

"Not for me, with me," he corrected.

"Whatever." Sloane would not argue about words and definitions. "I think you know what I mean."

"I do." Gene lifted his leg off hers. "I just want you to think about it. As for your lease, people break them all the time when it's for the right reasons. Living with the man you say you love seems like a pretty damn good reason to me."

Sloane bit her tongue. She wasn't very happy that he'd thrown this twist into their relationship right after they'd made love and she was most vulnerable to his smooth words. But she wouldn't succumb to this type of pressure.

"I wish I could just say I'll do this in the name of love," she told him, "but I have a very good job that I worked my butt off to get. As much as I'd like to partner up with you, professionally speaking, I can't just walk away from my work—and you should be able to understand that."

Gene's eyes steeled. "Can't or won't?"

She frowned. "It's the same thing. How dare you try to make me seem selfish or feel guilty?"

"That's not what I'm doing," he insisted, gazing up and down her body.

Sloane suddenly felt self-conscious lying there naked

while defending a position that he didn't seem to want to hear. She put a little space between them, using her hands to partially cover her breasts. "I earn a good living working at the Island Shores, including a first-rate health plan. Giving that up and trying to figure out how you can make up the difference makes no sense to me."

"I can't begin to compete with your salary and benefits at the Island Shores," Gene admitted. "But I can offer you what they never could, a home that would always be as much yours as mine, where we chart our course as a couple and let the future be our guide."

Sloane wasn't much in the mood to think about the future given the present circumstances that had them at odds, even if part of her was moved by the notion of a share-and-share-alike philosophy with the man she loved and wanted to believe truly loved her. But a greater part of her was reluctant to give in to something that almost seemed to be backing her into a corner that she did not want to be in.

"Sorry I brought it up," Gene grumbled in response to her stone-cold silence.

"I'm not sure you are," Sloane tossed at him. "Otherwise you would have given it more thought and seen that asking me to do this put me in a very awkward position." She peered at him. "I'd be happy to assist you at the B&B when you need an extra hand and Dayna can't cover it. But other than that—"

Gene's eyes narrowed. "Yeah, I get it. And, by the way, I wasn't looking for a damned assistant like Dayna, but an equal partner in every sense of the word. I actually thought this was something that might appeal to you. Obviously I was wrong. Just forget it."

"Like that's going to happen," she snorted. "I can't

simply put out of my mind your request and expect things to go back to how they were before."

"Nothing has to change," he said. "Certainly not on my part. This wasn't a deal breaker—just a way I wanted us to come together and build on what we have. If I overstepped my bounds, I'm sorry."

So am I, but what's done is done. Or was that an oversimplification of things? Sloane took a breath, meeting his eyes. "Can we talk about something else?"

"Sure." His brow furrowed. "Or maybe I should just get out of here so I don't end up sticking my foot in my mouth again."

Was he trying to run away when things got too hot for him? Is that what she had to look forward to in this relationship? Did they still have a relationship?

"If that's what you want," she said flatly and pulled the sheets up to cover her body.

"Probably better that way." He rolled out of bed and began to gather his clothes. "I'll dress outside, so you don't feel you need to cover up from me all of a sudden."

Sloane wanted to ask him to stay, but wasn't sure what the point was. He obviously had little interest in working through this. She watched him step into the living room and quickly dress as though he couldn't leave fast enough.

Sloane stood and slipped into a robe, walking out of the bedroom just as Gene approached the front door. As though sensing her, he turned around, a deadpan look on his face.

"I'll call you," he muttered, hesitated as if he wished to say something else, then left.

Sloane also found she had nothing to say and wondered if one sticking point was enough to undo a relationship that before tonight had shown nothing but promise and pleasure.

* * *

Gene drove home, wondering if he had blown it with Sloane by asking her to move in with him. He had honestly hoped she would fall in love with the idea as she had with him. Instead she had basically rejected it outright, clearly not interested in running the bed-and-breakfast with him. Not if it meant giving up her great job at the Island Shores.

What was I thinking, putting her on the spot like that? Maybe waiting till right after they'd made love with more intensity than ever wasn't the right time to approach the subject. Would there have ever been a right time? It seemed to him like her mind had already been made up from the start.

Gene was still pondering the wisdom of trying to mix matters of the heart with business when he retired to his suite. It obviously hadn't worked before in his life. Why on earth did he think it would be any different now with Sloane? Perhaps because they were in sync far more than had ever been the case with his ex-wife. He had assumed Sloane might be willing to take a leap of faith and raise the level of their love and commitment to new heights that could only strengthen their ties. He'd been wrong.

Maybe it had also been immature of him to react as he had by walking out instead of taking it like a man and showing her there were no hard feelings. He loved Sloane and didn't want to lose her. Certainly not over something that was never meant to make or break them as a couple. Had he already put a hole in their relationship that could never be repaired?

Gene reflected on those thoughts, feeling that no matter which way you looked at it, they both needed some time apart to chill and see where their relationship was headed.

* * *

A week had passed and Sloane had neither heard from Gene nor called him. She had admittedly been miserable in his absence, but wasn't surc he felt the same way. He'd indicated that her rejection of his asking her to live with him and operate the bed-and-breakfast was not going to make or break their relationship. Yet his silence made her seriously wonder if he'd been lying to her and himself.

Do I really even know him? Or was the sizzling romance between them just her fantasy?

Sloane sucked in a deep breath as she went for her morning run. It was the one thing she could count on for relaxation and pushing herself to the limit. The exercise also made her think about Gene and how he had come from nowhere to assist her when the sneaker wave knocked her onto her butt. They had taken that one moment in time and turned it into a romance that often left her head spinning and her heart aching for him.

She didn't want to see that all come to a crashing halt. And for what? Because she didn't jump for joy at the prospect of their personal and professional lives merging? She would have welcomed a marriage proposal as an indication that Gene was more committed to a lifetime with her than that she was merely someone to share the load in running his bed-and-breakfast. Yes, she had once been turned off at the thought of marriage slowing down her career goals. But that was then and this was now. Gene had made her want that type of official commitment of wedded bliss in which they could grow old together and maybe start a family. Apparently they were not on the same page in that regard, making it even more frustrating.

Sloane finished her run and took a shower before going to work. She did a few administrative tasks with her assistant, greeted some new arrivals, and went to meet with Alan to discuss guest services and next month's agenda. She sat in his office, along with other staff, trying to focus. But her mind kept returning to Gene.

"Do you love him more than your job?" Sloane recalled the direct question Gail had asked her. It was like comparing apples and oranges in many respects, as they were separate aspects of her life. Yet when it came right down to it, there was no doubt in Sloane's mind that her love for Gene trumped anything else, including working at the Island Shores. She couldn't deny it. Not the way her heart raced when he kissed her, made love to her, or even looked at her in a certain way.

But did that mean he had the right to ask her to quit her job and its security without any indication he was willing to put a ring on her finger? What if, heaven forbid, things didn't work out and she was left without the man and employment? The thought of Gene not being in her life made Sloane incredibly sad. Just as the thought of becoming Mrs. Malloy to pamper and spoil her man filled her with glee.

"Are you with us, Sloane?" She heard Alan's voice cut into her thoughts.

Sloane blinked and realized all eyes were on her. She quickly recovered, having kept up with the gist of the conversation. "Yes, I am," she said evenly.

"So what's your opinion?"

"I definitely think we should incorporate tour-guided trips to Hana into our premier guest services, with stops at Wailua Falls and Hamoa Beach a must!"

"I agree," Alan said. "Let's do it."

Sloane offered him a contented smile before again allowing her thoughts to drift off to Gene and what he had come to mean to her above and beyond the rewarding experience of working for the Island Shores.

* * *

That afternoon, Sloane had lunch with Kendra at an outdoor café in Kihei for some girl talk about the issues swirling in her head.

"You're kidding!" Kendra's eyes grew wide. "Gene actually asked you to quit your job?"

"More or less," Sloane responded, grabbing an onion ring.

"To move in with him and run the bed-and-breakfast?"

"Yes," Sloane reiterated.

"Wow." Kendra picked at steamed king crab legs. "And you turned him down?"

"I really wasn't sure what to say, since he caught me off guard. I told him it was unfair to ask me to do that." Sloane sighed. "At the time, I spoke with my head and not my heart."

"And I think he was speaking with his heart and not his head," Kendra said. "Which is a good thing, except it wasn't playing fair, even if he asked you for all the right reasons."

"I'm happy with my job, but I don't want to lose Gene because of it."

Kendra put down her fork. "You won't. Gene's smart enough to know a good thing when he has it."

Sloane rolled her eyes. "Right. Is that why I haven't heard a peep from him since he walked out of my condo a week ago?"

"I take it that means you haven't reached out either," Kendra surmised.

"I've wanted to a thousand times," Sloane confessed. "But I didn't want to say the wrong thing."

"I'm sure he feels the same way and that's why he hasn't picked up the phone. There is no wrong way to talk things through. But someone has to make the first move." Kendra met her gaze. "Maybe that someone should be you. Be the bigger person and get what you want—him."

"I do want him," Sloane uttered dreamily. She felt like she was suffocating without him around. She missed his touch, his smell, and the captivating sound of his voice.

"Then do something about it, short of giving up your career," Kendra said firmly. "After all, Gene's bed-and-breakfast was his vision, not yours. You're entitled to have your own separate career and still keep the relationship going strong."

"I want more than just to keep it going," Sloane said with a catch to her voice. "I'd really like to go the whole nine yards with him for the first time in my life."

Kendra's head snapped back. "You mean marriage?"

"Yes, I'm at that stage of my life—or relationship—where I want a ring, and I want him to put it there." She paused. "I'm just not sure he feels the same way."

"Maybe he doesn't think you're ready for marriage," Kendra suggested.

"He wouldn't know for sure unless he asked me," Sloane said, looking down at her sautéed scallions and tomato salsa. "But he wouldn't go down that road if marriage wasn't in the cards for him."

Kendra's brow creased. "So he's been married before. Big deal. Doesn't mean his mind is closed to ever marrying again. Not if someone like you came into his life and was open to the possibility and he was aware of it."

Sloane had to admit that both she and Gene had been vague on their thoughts about marriage. Had she given him the impression that it was totally off the table for her? Or was it the other way around? Did it matter at this point?

"I don't want to put any pressure on him," she stated.

Kendra laughed. "Right, like he hasn't put any pressure on you lately. I think you deserve to know where he stands and vice versa. It's the only way you can move forward for better or worse…in sickness or in health—"

Sloane couldn't help but grin at Kendra's clever words. She was nervous about what Gene might want out of their relationship beyond a live-in lover. Even if marriage was out of the question, maybe living together could work out as a way to remain a couple seriously committed to one another. Keeping her job was still important to Sloane, as Alan had shown faith in hiring her. She needed to honor that by not jumping ship prematurely. Surely Gene would understand that if he was half the man she believed him to be.

What if he wasn't? She needed to know so her love would not continue to go nowhere instead of to someone truly deserving of it.

Chapter 16

Gene placed plates and silverware in the dishwasher and got the kitchen back in order before stepping out into the rock garden for some fresh air. He realized it had been over a week since he'd seen Sloane. He had been hoping she would call, if only to say she missed him as much as he did her. But the phone was dead silent. Why? Had her love for him disappeared so easily, simply because he'd gone out on a limb and asked her something he now acknowledged was stupid? He should never have put her in a position of essentially choosing him or the job. He was doing just fine operating the bed-and-breakfast all by himself. He didn't need Sloane to partner up with him professionally or move into his house to make it complete. That wouldn't make him love her any more than he already did.

Sloane deserved the career she had worked hard for without him making her feel she was being selfish and not taking his needs into consideration. All he needed was her, pure and simple. And not just as his lover and a woman he loved being around.

Gene realized in a moment of clarity that what he wanted most was to make Sloane his wife. He loved her more than he could ever have thought possible. She had all the right ingredients to be his wife: beauty, brains, charm, sex appeal, common interests, humor and, yes, even independence. He was sure they could have a wonderful life together in a marriage built on love, trust and devotion. The onus was on him to do the right thing and convey these feelings to her. Hopefully it wasn't too late.

Would Sloane agree and be willing to put aside her hesitancy about tying the knot for fear of it interfering with her career aspirations? Would she reject his proposal as just another way for him to control her or try to push her into helping him run the bed-and-breakfast?

I can't let fear of failure stop me from opening my heart and soul to her. I hope she'll be able to see the sincerity in my eyes.

Gene took out his cell phone. He considered calling Sloane right then and there, but hesitated for fear that she might not want to talk to him given the difficult position he'd put her in and his childish behavior when they last saw each other. He had a much better idea to put himself out there and try to make amends in the best way he saw possible.

Sloane was a bundle of nerves as she stepped up to the front door of Malloy's Bed and Breakfast. She had swallowed her pride and was willing to make the first move in showing Gene how much she loved him and that she was more than willing to meet him halfway. Would agreeing to move in with him be enough to keep their relationship going strong?

Sloane stepped inside the house and could feel its warmth and allure all around her. She envisioned how she might put her own stamp on the place to truly become a part of it as Gene's live-in lover, even if she would have little to no role in the bed-and-breakfast side of things.

"Aloha." Sloane heard the voice and turned to see Dayna smiling at her.

Sloane smiled back at the woman whom Gene seemed so appreciative of for her contribution in helping to keep the B&B running smoothly. "Aloha, Dayna."

"You must be looking for Gene."

Sloane nodded. "Yes. Is he here?"

Dayna shook her head. "Afraid not. He had an errand to run."

"I see." *Now what? Do I wait for him to return?*

"I'm not sure when he'll be back," Dayna said. "But I'll tell him you dropped by."

"Mahalo," Sloane said, hiding her disappointment. She wanted to talk to Gene face to face rather than by phone.

Dayna surprised Sloane by taking her hand. "Gene loves you," she said gently. "Whatever is causing the strain on your relationship, just know that his heart is pure and his intentions honorable."

"I appreciate that." Sloane wanted to believe every word, but still needed to hear it from Gene.

"Don't give up on him," Dayna said, patting her hand. "After his divorce, Gene was a lost soul when it came to romance and connecting with someone who was truly his match. But you opened his eyes and helped him find love again and the possibilities it could bring to his life and yours. Go home and wait for him. He will make certain you don't regret it."

Sloane felt moved to give her a hug as she held back

tears. "Thank you," she whispered. Her thoughts were on Gene and where they might go from here.

When Sloane arrived at her condo, she found Gene standing there. She could barely hide her surprise. He had a serious look on his handsome face and gave her the benefit of a steady gaze with those deep gray-brown eyes.

"Hi," he said.

"Hi." She looked at him, feeling her heart beating rapidly. "I just came from your place."

"I know. Dayna told me."

"She never said you were—"

"I didn't tell her exactly where I was going," Gene said. He moved his arm from behind his back to reveal a dozen roses. "These are for you."

Sloane took them and bent down to smell the fragrant flowers. She had been so focused on him that she'd missed what he was hiding behind his back. "They're lovely. Thank you."

A smile formed on his lips. "It's just my way of saying I'm sorry."

Was he? Could they get past it now and move on? She smiled at him hopefully. "So am I." More than he knew. She hadn't wanted anything to come between them.

"You have nothing to be sorry for," Gene insisted. "It's all on me. I was wrong to put that kind of pressure on you, and I don't want it to hang over us."

Neither did Sloane. Not when he meant so much to her. She looked at him and felt a sigh of relief. She realized they were still standing outside her door. "Would you like to come in?"

"Yes, I'd love to," he said eagerly.

Inside, Sloane set the roses down. She loved roses and it meant a lot to get them from Gene. But they still had to deal with the issue that had nearly ruined their relationship. She hoped that her remedy would work for him and everything else would fall back into place.

"Would you like a drink?" she offered.

He stood tall. "Maybe later. Right now, I'd like to talk to you."

Sloane nodded. "Okay. But first, there's something I want to say."

"I'm listening..."

She sucked in a deep breath and forced herself not to avert her eyes. "I've been thinking about what you said and, if the offer still stands, I'd like to move in with you. Not as your business partner, but as your woman. I love you, Gene, and want us to have a life together."

Gene held her gaze in silence, causing Sloane's pulse to race with uneasiness. Would he balk at her suggestion?

"I want that, too," he said coolly. "I accept your offer to live with me, but it comes with a caveat—"

She locked eyes with him. "What's that?"

Gene paused, staring into her beautiful dark eyes. "I want you to marry me," he said unwaveringly.

Sloane had to digest the words. "You're proposing..."

A grin lifted his cheeks. He took a box out of his pocket and handed it to her. "Open it."

She opened the box and saw a glittering three-stone diamond ring. Dazzled by it, Sloane was practically frozen in place as Gene removed the ring from the box. He took her hand, fell to one knee and put the ring on her finger. She gazed down at him, shaking.

"Will you please marry me, Sloane?" he said. "I know I messed up before, but now I know what truly would make me the happiest man on Maui and probably the whole world. That's you, Sloane. I want us to spend the rest of our lives together discovering different ways to fulfill one another. I don't give a damn if you work at the Island Shores from now on, and that's the truth. The bed-and-breakfast can continue to function fine as is. I just want you as my wife, lover and best friend." He paused, looking up into her eyes. "Say yes..."

Sloane put her quivering hand up to her mouth in absolute bliss. Her dream had come true in a few incredible moments that she would remember for the rest of her life. A life she now had someone to share with as husband and wife.

"Yes, Gene Malloy," she cried. "I will marry you."

"Mahalo, darling." His face brightened. "We'll be so good for each other."

"I agree wholeheartedly." Sloane grinned and her eyes glistened with tears of joy. "You can get up now and kiss me like you mean it."

Gene rose to his feet. He put his arms around her waist, drawing her oh so near. "I can do that and show you without a shadow of a doubt that I meant every word I said."

Sloane melted into his arms and absorbed the powerful kiss that took control of her mind, body and, most of all, her heart.

* * * * *